MEDITATIONS ON THE MOTHER TONGUE

STORIES BY AN TRAN

C&R Press
Conscious & Responsible

Cover Art: "Throttled Infrastructure" and "Two Face 2" by Eugenia Loli
Interior design by DaQuan Sims
Exterior design by C&R Press

Printed in the United States of America

First Edition
1 2 3 4 5 6 7 8 9

Library of Congress Cataloging-in-Publication Data

ISBN: 978-1-936196-71-5
LCCN: 2016950661

C&R Press
Conscious & Responsible
www.crpress.org
Winston-Salem, NC 27104

For special discounted bulk purchases, please contact:
C&R Press sales@crpress.org
Contact lharms@crpress.org to book events, readings and author signings.

MEDITATIONS
ON THE MOTHER TONGUE

STORIES BY AN TRAN

There is nothing here that's not been said before,
Nor have I any skill in the craft of composition.
I do not expect this to be of much benefit to others;
I write only to perfume my own mind.

-Santideva

Contents

Meditations on the Mother Tongue

I.

She is so small and thin, standing barely over five feet, dressed plainly in a yellow tank top and dark gray sweatpants. He wonders, what could she possibly know of parkour? But when she moves, all the traceurs stop to watch. They circle her, staring. She floats over the obstacles no one else can climb. When any of the others jump, they must punch their legs into the ground. When Cordy jumps, it is as if gravity has simply released its hold on her. And Bao knows that Cordy can teach them flight.

He stands nervously as she appraises him and the sequence he'd just demonstrated. It is only two vaults across a handicapped ramp's brick walls, but he keeps crashing into the second wall. Her face is long, eyes moving from Bao to the ramp and back again. She nods and then walks forward, waving him over to her. He goes the long way, taking the steps beside the ramp.

Cordy says, "Your take-off is sloppy."

Bao rebuts, "I didn't stutter this time. Managed the kong. It can't be the take-off."

She shakes her head. "Not your legs. Your arms. You need to jump with your arms too. Here, watch." She squats in front of him. As she descends, her arms swing down in an arc until they are stretched behind her, like a hen folding her wings at rest. Then Cordy jumps, her whole body unfurling open until she is stretched straight. "You can't just jump with your legs," she says after landing. "It's like you're a spring; your whole body has to explode to launch you into the air." She repeats the movement slowly. "Watch my arms," she instructs. Cordy squats and jumps over and over.

Bao studies, following the arc of her arms down and up and down again. He glances at the other boys for only a moment and sees the swing of their arms with every jump. "Okay," he says, nodding. "I think I've got it." He gestures for Cordy to move aside. He takes a breath. This time, he concentrates on swinging his arms. This time, it feels like he is floating into the air, not leaping, as if he has until the limits of time to consider his path, to make adjustments. The first vault sends him flying higher and faster than he thought possible, high enough over the second wall that he only needs to set his hands down below him and nudge himself forward to return to the ground. And though he hadn't known anyone was watching, all the traceurs and traceuses roar in congratulations.

He turns around and sees Cordy smiling, her palms pressed together as if in prayer. She says, "Great! But you know it doesn't count. Once is nothing."

Bao nods. A new skill is not considered learned until it's been done at least three times. "Once is nothing," he repeats.

***

Under Cordy's instruction, Bao watches a documentary titled *Parkour: Generations*. It follows the first traceurs—David Belle, his cousins Williams Belle and Chau Belle Dinh—as they scramble over the architecture of Lisses, France. An hour into the film, to Bao's delight, there is a scene of Chau speaking in Vietnamese to his mother, a short and plump woman with her hair—black with streaks of gray and white—tied into a pony tail. She wears a black floral print dress. Around her neck is a gold chain from which a large jade Buddha pendant hangs. Behind her, a kitchen sink is filled with porcelain plates and bowls and a forest of chopsticks. Pinned to a wall is a bright red poster board, a stack of calendar sheets stapled to the bottom. Printed on the poster board is an extravagant painting of a female buddha in a white and gold dress, standing on a large lotus platform. It looks very much like how Bao's mother has ornamented their own kitchen.

The scene is short. At first, Bao tries to cover up the subtitles, but there are too many words he doesn't know. When did he forget his first language? He is forced to read the text.

Chau says to his mother: *Ma, can you tell the camera how you feel about this? The jumping thing I do with David and my brother?*

His mother replies, *I am scared every day for the both of you.*

One evening, Bao shows his own mother the video clip. She lies on the couch, the television on, and he kneels on the ground like a knight, holding open his laptop atop one knee. He tries to explain the sport's ties back to Viet Nam. She glances from time to time from the television to the computer screen and back. Ma says, "So it like kung fu, but you only jump away? Like rabbit?"

He frowns and answers, "I guess that's one way to look at it." He says, "Look, Raymond Belle spent six years in Da Lat before he moved to Paris."

"Đà Lat," Ma corrects. He tries to repeat after her. She laughs. "Accent con much heavy than Phuc's." Her eyes are fixed again to the television; she speaks without looking at him.

"Thicker," he corrects her. "My accent's thicker than Phuc's. But I'm learning to move like the Vietnamese."

She says, "How nice. That is good for you. Everybody need hobby." She yawns.

Bao says nothing. He turns away sulking. It isn't clear to him what he expected or wanted. Normally he and his brother try not to bother Ma when she's home from work. She isn't home often—she works two jobs—and there is always a terrible sense of guilt for disturbing her rest. He goes up the stairs and into his brother's room; they watch re-runs of an old sitcom together. They used to sit on the ground at the foot of the bed, their heads cranked upward at an old gray television. They played story-based games, up to 80 hours long, and whoever wasn't playing would read the scrolling text aloud.

The television in Phuc's room was beside the door into the hall. Sometimes, when the door was left open and they were playing their games, Bao would see, out of the corner of his eye, a woman in a dress standing in the hall. She was a gentle blue glow of a woman, normally facing Ma's closed bedroom door. Sometimes she looked at him. Sometimes she walked back and forth in the hall. When Bao looked straight on, she normally vanished immediately. She was his personal secret for ages, the Blue Lady who watched over them.

He turns to Phuc now and asks, "Do you ever still see the Blue Lady?"

Phuc scrunches his face up for a moment. He shrugs and says, "Not in a long time."

"Do you think she's still here? Do you think we made her up?"

"We never told each other we saw her until you were already in college. That can't be made up. I think we just got older. You know how they say kids are more sensitive to ghosts? I think that's it."

"Yeah, that must be it."

***

The traceurs spend the first two hours of every Saturday session absorbed in the conditioning of their bodies. They line up with their backs against a wall, inverted onto their hands. Then, they lower themselves until their lips can touch the concrete and press themselves back up with labored grunts. They are not permitted to play on the grounds until they complete fifty consecutive press-ups from their handstands, then cross the concrete in a quadrupedal walk for three hundred feet, and lastly broad jump a short eight-foot gap three hundred times.

Too many times, Bao wants to give up and go home. His muscles are giving out. Every breath feels like a draw of acid in his lungs. Lakes of sweat form near his eyes and blurs out his vision. To endure the pain, he chants quietly, *"Être fort pour être utile. Être fort pour être utile."* This is what Cordy says to anyone who complains about the conditioning or asks her why there must be so much hard work before they can play. *Be strong to be useful.*

She had once told him that physical fitness is a moral duty, that parkour is the realization of that duty. Bao is on his hands and his feet, crawling across the concrete. His palms hurt, having to hold his weight up against sand, small pebbles, and shards of glass. He is shaking. He brings her voice to mind. He reminds himself that the consequence of failure is weakness, that weakness is not useful, that if an emergency were to strike at this very moment, people would be hurt because he isn't strong enough. Now he growls. He pushes through the pain. He endures it in the name of strength. He whispers, "I dedicate my strength to all of humanity, to my community, to my family." He whispers this again and again. The mantra becomes his font of willpower.

By dusk, the plaza is strewn with bodies lying exhausted and panting over the sun-warmed bricks. Overhead, bands of light stretch across opposite horizons like threads of sinew. Bao and Cordy lie at a distance from the others, side by side. Cordy says, "I heard you chanting. It's a good idea. You should start making everyone do it."

"Wait, what? *I* should start?" He turns his head toward her, his cheek pressed against the brick ground. She looks at him, but doesn't respond. "Oh. Right. The semester's almost over. You're going back to France."

Cordy still says nothing.

"What are we supposed to do after you're gone?"

She answers this time. "You spread the gospel. You teach everyone that parkour without altruism is meaningless."

His eyes flash toward the community for a moment. Some have stood again, speaking softly to each other. He says quietly, "They won't listen to me. They just want to have fun and climb on things."

She says, "You'll teach them to respect their elders. Raymond Belle's parkour is the only parkour."

He sighs, turning away, making rakes of his fingers that he forces through his hair. "It'll be a lot of work. I can't do it on my own."

She tells him, "Don't be a selfish jerk. You're supposed to be strong."

He laughs.

II.

The class was small, only eight students minus a pair on the registry that never showed up. The instructor didn't write her name on the board, but it sat high on the header of her syllabi: *Jennifer Lam, MA.* She was a young woman, probably raised in North America if not born. The other students were mostly Vietnamese too. During the recitations, Bao fixed his eyes on the floor. The students all stumbled over the syllables as they spoke, their voices soft and clumsy.

There was one woman who wasn't Vietnamese, Tara. When the students took turns introducing themselves, hers was the only story that differed. "I'm a historian who studies biochemical weapons," she said. "I'd like to read and maybe translate what Vietnamese historians have written about Agent Orange."

Bao caught Tara after class outside the doors of the building. "Hey," he said. "Really cool reason to be taking the class."

She smiled. "Oh, thanks! I felt really out of place, actually."

"We all do," admitted Bao. "Did you notice? We all stammer like we're being made to walk the plank."

Tara laughed. "No, not at all! Maybe I don't know enough of the language yet." And then she pointed to the graphic on his t-shirt, a logo of the letters *PKVA* in blue, set beside the silhouette of an airborne man with his limbs flared. She asked, "You do parkour?"

He answered, "Not in a couple years, but I did for a long time." The community consisted now of only thrill-seekers and teenaged daredevils looking to make it as stuntmen or obstacle course competitors, like Bao had predicted years ago. There was no one left who cared about being useful. "Close to a decade," he added.

Tara exclaimed, "That's awesome! I had an ex that always wanted to learn."

Bao smiled. "It's easier than it looks."

"Can you teach me?" She asked with a smile.

"So you can show him up?" They laughed. "Yes, of course, I can. I will. There's this plaza we used to go to. I'll give you directions. Are you free Saturday morning?"

***

One of Ms. Lam's early classes focused on the different names for family members, all words Bao knew intimately: Ma was mother, *Ba* was father, *Anh* was brother, *Chi* was sister. He knew how the words for grandparent, uncle and aunt differed between the mother's side and the father's side. The class went on for three hours, the students chanting basic sentences, a bore for Bao. His mind couldn't help but to wander, and he found himself comparing Vietnamese words against their English counterparts.

Ba was also the word for 'three.' Family members were seldom called by name; numbers had a magic property and every person had a designation. Bao was the older brother, called *Anh Hai*, or 'the second brother.' Phuc, *Anh Ba*, 'the third brother,' was two years younger. Bao had uncles and aunts he never learned the names of, only knowing them as Uncle Eight, Aunt Six, and so forth.

When the class arrived at the six variations of the word *ma*, Bao thought about how, in Vietnamese, the words for 'mother' and 'ghost' were distinguished only through pitch; the former was sang in high jubilation, while the latter was a despondent drone.

He listened carefully to his voice. He tried singing the words in falsetto, and next growling them from the belly. He tried facing different directions for each recitation. Nothing made any difference; he only ever heard himself say one word.

***

They began slowly, Bao and Tara. It made him feel young

again, made him recall the Saturday mornings he'd spent here in his college youth, Cordy instructing him in the ways of movement and its marriage to altruism. It felt exactly the same, though his joints began aching sooner now as an adult. The bricks in the plaza had lost their vibrancy, now a pinkish hue. The concrete was scarred with fissures at the corners, weeds sprouting up through the cracks.

Bao taught Tara first how to land, how to let the force of gravity close the hinges of her legs into a squat, and next how to jump. He taught her how to roll from one shoulder to the opposite hip and, over the weeks, the entire vocabulary of vaults and how they applied in a run. "You learn fast," he told her one day. "Faster than I did."

She beamed. She said, "*Cảm ơn, anh.*"

"Of course," he replied. "You're welcome. Thanks for getting me out here again." He hopped up onto the first wall of the handicapped ramp, and rested there facing her. He took a deep breath. It'd been too easy to forget how much he missed all of this—the sun warming his back, the stillness spreading over his mind before a jump, the gentle pain of the city's stone skin scuffing and scratching his own.

Tara stepped forward to the ramp. Bao inched to the side to give her room. She jumped. Her waist collided with the wall's edge; she bounced and fell back to the ground. She said, "*Tôi không được*"—she paused, scrunched her face, and then finished her sentence in English—"jump that high."

"*Nhảy* is jump," said Bao. "And be careful about saying the word '*I*.'"

"Why?"

"I'm sure Ms. Lam will go over it in class eventually. '*I*' and '*you*' are like dirty words a lot of the time. I don't know why, really." He shrugs. "In polite conversation, you only use third person. You don't call attention to yourself."

***

Tara asked one day, after their session, "Do you know what I don't get?"

They lay strung out on the pavement, staring at the sky, the same way Bao remembered all his training sessions ending so many years before. He replied to her with an inquisitive hum.

"Blue," she said. "I don't get 'blue.'"

He said, "*It's xanh.*"

"But that's green," she argued. "Why do you use the same word for two colors?"

He laughed. He wondered the same thing as a child, and even asked once. Bao's mother used to put on a Vietnamese television series, an adaptation of *Journey to the West*, that he and Phuc watched while she tended to house chores on Sundays. When the monk and the monkey had emerged from a forest, the camera panned over an open field with richly green grass and an open blue sky overhead. Bao called loudly into the kitchen where his mother was cleaning the stove and asked her how the Vietnamese distinguished between green and blue. Ma answered, "We just say, *xanh like the sky, or, xanh like leaves.*"

Now he answered Tara, "They're the same color. Just different shades."

Tara responded, "I don't get it. That doesn't make sense."

He told her, "I don't think they ever learn it as its own thing. Like, as an independent color. Blue just doesn't exist."

III.

Tham says, "You're stressing out too much. *Trời đất*, look at your hands! You're gripping the wheel too hard. Your fingers are glowing red."

She's right. All Bao can feel in his fingers is a hot sting where the joints should be. He lets up his grip. He takes a deep breath. "Sorry," he says.

"Don't apologize," she responds, gently touching his shoulder. "I'm sorry this stresses you out."

"Why are *you* apologizing?" he asks.

"Because I feel bad for you. And I don't know what it's like. I had really great parents."

"I didn't have bad parents," Bao retorts.

He realizes he's coming up too quickly on the car ahead and brakes hard. Their car drops in speed, forces them into lurching forward in their seats. "Sorry about that," he says.

"I didn't mean it like that, *anh*," Tham says. She tries again in Vietnamese: "*Có nghĩa là tôi không có buồn vì cha mẹ tôi đã phải làm việc rất nhiều.*" She meant, I was never sad because of my parents working so much. "My parents weren't around either, but you grew up here. Back home, work is how parents show their love. It is pure selflessness to work hard and to provide. You wanted something they didn't know how to give."

"I know they tried their hardest," he says, noticing again the ache in his fingers. He releases his right hand from the wheel, opens it all the way, tries to stretch out the pain. Then he closes it into a tight fist. Then he shakes it loose and returns it to the wheel.

"Yes," agrees Tham. "If your mother didn't care, she

wouldn't have arranged our marriage."

Bao chuckled. "Ma arranged our marriage because I was letting our *dai gia dình* down by not contributing to the next generation."

Tham says, "You're wrong. She wanted to see your children before the dementia set in, *anh*."

"Too late for that, aren't we?" Bao's mother has been degrading for years now, her attempts to recall a memory leaping over larger and larger gaps the way audio skips from a scratched disc. He and Phuc put her in a skilled nursing facility eight months back. "It shouldn't matter anymore," he says.

Tham asks, "So why does it?" When he doesn't answer, she giggles. "*Má anh* is right about you, you know? You just like to argue everything."

"I'm not arguing," he says.

"What do you call it, then?"

"I am calmly explaining to you why you're wrong."

Out of the corner of his eye, he sees Tham grinning at him. She asks, "Try that again in *tiếng Việt*."

Bao laughs and shakes his head. It isn't possible, not politely.

She pokes him in the side. "Now you understand, don't you, *anh*?"

***

The room is small, the size of a walk-in closet. The wallpaper is an offensive yellow, a color like aged parchment. A small window sits in the wall across from the door, the glass filmed with dust. Ma wears a green hospital gown, lies propped up in her bed watching a television that is fixed into a high corner.

Bao stands in the doorway, knocks gently on the frame, says loudly, "*Thưa má, con trai Bảo ở đậy. Má có khoẻ không?*" Please, Mother. The child Bao is here. Are you doing well?

Tham enters behind him. As soon as she's through the door, she falls to her knees, her palms pressed together and held to her forehead as if in prayer. She bends at the hips, touches her forehead to the ground, repeats the bow twice more before rising. Already, she's venerating Ma as an elder ready to pass, on the verge of becoming an ancestor worthy of worship.

Ma looks at Bao. She doesn't smile. Her face is pruned in wrinkles; her hair is thin, dark gray like storm clouds. She says, "*Bao và Tham, ha? Khoẻ.*" She asks in English, "How you kids doing?"

She's lucid. She remembers him. Bao sighs heavily, and then realizes he'd held his breath since crossing through the door.

Tham nods to Ma and says, *Vâng cảm ơn cô, tụi con khoẻ.*"Yes, thank you. We are well.

Hanging from Bao's hooked fingers is a plastic bag containing rice and tofu he'd brought from home. He crosses the room to a small table beneath a window and unpacks the food. He gazes through the window to a small courtyard with a white fountain, a walkway of red Virginia clay winding around it. There are gowned elders meandering about, or else sitting still on benches. Across the courtyard, a set of steps leads to the entrance doors. To the right of the steps is a shallow wheelchair ramp, braced by brass rails on either side. A dozen routes map themselves in his mind, playful paths he would've leapt through in his youth. Bao's body still remembers, bombarding him with aching pleas to jump again.

"*Anh,*" calls Tham. He turns around.

Ma's kicking her blankets off, green sheets now billowing everywhere like drapery. She stands up out of bed and faces the door, the sheets sloppily curtaining her shoulders, falling over and around her like a monk's robes. She says, "*Cần phải về nhà. Hai đứa con đang ở nhà một mình.*" I need to get home. My two boys are there alone.

Bao turns around and watches. Part of him thinks he should go to her, assure her he's there, assure her of when and where she is. He tries to sort through the vocabulary, but can't find the right words. In Vietnamese, there is no such thing as tense, no good way to lace words into a frame of time. He grunts quietly, and looks again out the window. He speaks into the glass, tells Tham, "Let her get up. Walk around. She won't go far."

Tham replies sternly, "No, *anh,* I'm not worried about that. *Má anh sẽ chết sớm. Anh cần phải chuyển nghiệp của anh.*"

It takes him a moment to understand such a long sentence, for his mind to untangle the string of sounds. As soon as its meaning is revealed to him, Bao grits his teeth. You need to transfer your karma to her. He once heard that as one approaches death, the karmic fruit of a life ripens. The mind recalls the fruit of highest priority; how the mind responds determines the next birth. To attach too deeply to regrets means rebirth in a hell realm, means to wander a painful memory as a hungry ghost again and again, maybe for millennia, until the karma has exhausted. And, for the Vietnamese, the cessation of mind is death. The body is only residue.

Tham says, "Anh, you need to talk to her. *Hoặc má anh sẽ trở thành ma.*" Or your mother will be a ghost.

Bao sighs. He doesn't yet move. In the courtyard, there's a squirrel on one of the rails of the ramp. It dashes down the length, leaps to the other rail, immediately pounces up from its landing to the wayward branch of a tree. For a moment, he thinks of Cordy. An ache begins to warm in his knees. From behind, Tham scolds, "You're being selfish, *anh.*"

Bao winces. He sighs again and nods. "I know. You're right," he admits, slowly crossing the room toward his mother. "I'm supposed to be stronger than this." Now standing in the doorway before Ma, Bao lowers himself to his knees, hands clasped to his forehead, bowing to the ground three times. He breathes only once for each, a long exhaust of air folding down, a slow drink of it coming up. It occurs to him, curled over on the floor, that there is no progression in a Vietnamese life, only a sequence of generations replacing each other. A child is always a child; a parent is always the elder. From the ground, Ma's body is a green tower. Bao stands up. He takes her hands into his. Her skin is dry, wrinkled and broken. It feels like sandpaper, like grit and earth.

There isn't any reason to tell her when she is. There isn't any way to do it either. But he can leave her a son who speaks her language, who knows she left her love at home when she left at all.

He says to his Ma, "*Con Bao đây.*" Your child is right here.

A Clear Sky Above the Clouds

The Americans are in Sumatra because Teuku put a video he took of an otter running into the cave on Youtube a year ago. Dr. Schweyer thinks it may be the hairy-nosed otter although everyone knows that creature has not existed on the island of Sumatra for a hundred years. And so she asked if Teuku might lead her and the scientists to the cave and help her see if the beast still lives. Teuku's father insisted on accompanying too, on account of Teuku being only thirteen. His father also warned the Americans that because the monsoon soon begins, they can only be away for fourteen days. Dr. Schweyer agreed to the conditions and Teuku recalls the intensity of her grin, the way her face formed rounded lines like a frame to display her lips and how Dr. Schweyer said, "Thank you thank you thank you! This could change the world." Teuku wonders now how an otter could change the world. What significance could a creature that is likely dead hold for the planet?

Their steps echo from both ahead and behind, a flutter of pitter-patters from their feet matting against hardened dirt and ragged stone. There is chatter, whispers amplified in the rocky tunnel, which Teuku absorbs eagerly and silently. They talk about their lives. It feels very much to Teuku an odd topic of conversation, snaking through the cavern in the dark. They departed their lives at the cavern's mouth, far back through the stretch of darkness and back to sunlight. Down here, they are empty. Still, the Americans converse lightly and Teuku imagines their voices bouncing around at the surface of the world, ping-ponging off the round edges of the cave's opening, far away from this subterranean place, this deep other-world inside a rocky face by the river.

Dr. Schweyer and her two colleagues do not look the way Teuku imagines scientists to look. On the TV, they wear white coats that fan out behind them like capes. However, she and the two men are dressed in t-shirts and shorts and hiking boots. The white man, Fred, is rounder than anyone Teuku has ever seen and the black man, Lucas, is lanky and long-limbed, stretched to a giant's height. He towers over Teuku's father like a tree.

Teuku is hypnotized by the music of the cave, the way it accompanies human speech. A voice emerges small and then bounces off cavern walls, splits into a chorus that comes from all around, its vibration like warm electricity on the skin. It is a reverent hymn and he follows every word like scripture.

"What's strange," says Dr. Schweyer, "is that otters aren't cave-dwellers. I can't see a reason why one would run for this cave to begin with."

"Maybe they've been forced down here by the deforestation," suggests Fred.

"Is there food?" asks Dr. Schweyer.

Lucas bends down and picks a coiled shell from the ground. A bundle of prickly legs retracts into the spiral. "Hermit crabs. There's definitely food."

His father announces, "Here" as they step into a part of the cave where the walls have stretched apart. Slowly, he drags the beam of his flashlight across the cleared ground. Ancient bones stained orange and brown and black jut out from the floor. "My God," says Dr. Schweyer. "What the hell is living down here?" Many of the bones look broken and are scattered randomly. Dr. Schweyer aims her light into a depression in the cave floor. A rounded bone protrudes. "Is that what I think it is?"

Teuku does not know what she thinks it is, but watches her carefully as she approaches it, kneels and scoops away the mud around it. She starts laughing. Lucas and Fred do too. Teuku takes a step closer to inspect her discovery. He sees that the bone is large and cone-shaped. There is a hole in it, a socket. And now Teuku sees. It is a skull submerged into the cavern, a single eye peeking out from the earth.

***

In the days that pass, Teuku learns that the cave drains the waters from the forest, that the rock and mud washed into the cave bury the bones and then harden over time into rock. Because of this, the skull may be perfectly whole, protected by layers of rock. Dr. Schweyer—who insists on Abbey now—is very excited; she says that the skull is recent and if they can excavate it to see if the brow is round or flat, they can know if the hairy-nosed otter still lives. Or at least, she said, lived more recently than they had thought. Other bones are excavated piecemeal over the next days. They are tagged like gifts. Colored tickets are tied to each fragment by string and arranged on a long table inside a tent. The Americans have pitched round tents for the team to sleep in and larger house-shaped tents to work in. Teuku must adjust to sleeping inside a cloth tube. It's a restrictive thing like a bandage. All wrapped up, Teuku has no freedom to move. When he wakes in the mornings, he springs out of his tent and opens up each of his many aching joints, spreading himself wide to the world.

Breakfast is prepared by Fred—always a couple slices of salami and a piece of bread. Teuku and his father split their share; it is too much in the morning for their stomachs. Abbey sits with Teuku for an hour or two before going into the cave. She wants to know stories of Sumatra. She asks, "How do you cope with all the rain? Does it make you sad, so many days without the sun?"

Teuku nods. "Yes. It can make all of us sad. It is difficult to eat. We subsist mostly on the durians the wind blows down from the trees. So it is dark and you are hungry and you are sad." Now he smiles at her. "We have a saying here, that there is always a clear sky above the clouds." He points a finger up at Mt. Kerinci and the way the spire pierces through the sheet of sky. "And so we know that the sun will always return and we can think of what it is like up high."

***

Later, the team dives again into the cave. They follow a trail of extension cords that wind back to a gasoline-powered generator at the camp. There is light at the other end. Bright yellow bulbs stand on tripod towers. In the dig site clearing, it smells of mold. The rain water of the forest drains into here and lingers. The rocky walls glisten in the lamp glow. The acoustics of the cave produce the music of dripping water. The clearing has been mapped in a grid of twine.

Tomorrow, more Americans will arrive to help the excavation. Teuku is told there is much digging to be done; he offers to help, but Abbey says that it is a precise digging—mathematical—and so he must watch her and learn for a few days first. After that, he is only permitted to soften the stone surrounding the skull. He is never to dig himself. Teuku's father spends the days wandering the forest with Fred, who cannot dig because of his back. Together, they set up camera traps around the camp site in order to photograph any remaining otters. Teuku enjoys it inside, enjoys watching Abbey and Lucas sweat and labor in the dim light. Lucas makes smiling flirtatious comments by the hour. He digs shirtless so that his browned skin sheens as much as the cavern walls in the electric light. He peeks at Abbey, trying to catch the eye that she never passes his way. Her attention is always downward, at the earth that has swallowed the otter's skull. She devotes herself to breaking apart the mineralized ground. Teuku imagines her searching, always searching. Lately, he dreams of Abbey digging into his mind. He cannot explain why, but it feels as if poisoned flowers have bloomed inside him when he thinks of her.

***

Over several days, Teuku hears a percussive drumming tunneling through to the team from deeper within the cave. The advent of the other Americans—Abbey calls them interns—makes the sound more frequent, more urgent. He cannot seem to describe it. It is a sound like a falling durian—the thwack as it hits a tree's root, the way all the spikes splinter before the shell splits. But it is also a sound that melts as it reaches Teuku's ears, and he does not have better words. He does not know how a sound can melt. When he asks Abbey, she tells him it is the sound of their digging tools traveling deep into the cave and then coming back. That is why, she explains, the melting sound comes more often with the interns here. Teuku does not believe her.

One day, as the scientists and interns busy themselves with bones and digging, Teuku takes a flashlight deeper. Maybe he can chase the sound before it melts.

As he wanders through the labyrinth of cavern tunnels, he thinks carefully about Abbey's focus. It is bizarre to him. In the evenings, when the scientists and interns and even Teuku's father celebrate by campfire, sharing stories of adult matters and the bottled lagers the interns brought in crates by Jeep, Abbey recedes to the skeletal tent. The other night, Teuku observed her poring over the bones, scribbling notes out on a yellow legal pad. Above her head, a brown moth fluttered in orbit around an electric lantern that was hoisted upon a steel post. The flickering shadow of the moth's wings strobed the light so that it seemed Abbey's movements jerked in frames. Hand left, hand right, left, right. Nothing else moved.

Teuku's heart panged in sympathy for her, this brilliant young woman who struggled with such desperation to reach out and touch another species. She wore the same face when she stared at the bones as when she left the skeletal tent for her own, stealing a glance at Teuku and then at the campfire and the joyous crowd. It was an expression of longing and of puzzlement. Teuku could measure by Abbey's gaze how far she felt from each, her peers and her discovery—the gap to the living was far greater, her own species more alien.

***

In fifteen minutes of walking, Teuku's feet already ache from the pressure of stones. The surface is less forgiving here, with jagged spikes and pointed slopes. The floor is mottled with rocky abrasions. Perhaps his soles are bruised. It is cooler down here though. The water that drains in from the outside comes in the form of thin streams twisting together into a braid.

The sound is louder now; it is no longer a drumming. Now it is solid. It has a tune like a growl. No, like a grunt. Like a voice. Like voices emerging from the throat of the cave. But it is dark. It is so dark that the insects that cling to the rock walls are white. Everywhere, the walls are frosted with insects like flakes. They scatter away from the beam of the flashlight. Teuku thinks this is not normal. This is the other-world, where insects run from light. He is not scared though. His life waits for him outside; it is safe, far away from this inner world.

Teuku recognizes these sounds. He has heard them before. They sing off-key; the tune pulsates to an awkward rhythm like all the accents are taking place between his heartbeats. They take place somewhere in the space between a chirp and a clatter; these are otters.

They will hide from him; Teuku knows this. He wonders how they came down here. Perhaps there is another opening to the surface somewhere, another extension of the river. He calls ahead of himself. His voice volleys around in the cavern chambers.

The tunnel curves up ahead. The beam of his flashlight illuminates the wall. Blue mushrooms curl out of fissures in the rock. The walls are splotched with these growths. A stone flies from beyond the curve by Teuku's nose and slaps against rock. He stops. They are running away, deeper. He must turn back.

***

Abbey is again in the tent tonight, scribing notes and measuring the plaster casts Fred took earlier. Around the campfire, Teuku's father drinks beers with Lucas. Fred is speaking to a spectacled intern, a thin and mousy man with cropped brown hair fashioned up like blades of grass. Teuku sits beside them, warming his hands by the fire. The sky rumbles softly; another storm is coming, but they still have a few days before the work is washed away.

Fred has a galloping sort of laugh that rolls out from his stomach. They are speaking of Abbey. "I've known her a long time," he says. "Don't you worry about her." He clinks his bottle to the intern's. They both drink.

The young man props his forearms up on his knees and looks down at the fire. "She's bossy, isn't she?"

Fred's face grows grave, features falling such that even the fat roundness of his cheeks does little to powder his complexion with jolly. "Abbey's a brilliant woman, son. More so than I am and she's half my age. A guy acts the way she does, he's called driven. But Abbey or any other woman is just a bitch. Something's wrong with that, right?" Fred shrugs and laughs again. "I pick her brain much as I can. But you try socializing with her yet? It's a fiasco." Now he looks at Teuku. "What do you two talk about every morning anyway?"

Teuku blinks. "Oh. I tell her stories of Sumatra. She asks questions."

"Anything to do with our hairy friend?"

Teuku shakes his head. "Very little."

"How interesting," replies Fred, his eyes back to the fire. It feels to Teuku like the letters of Fred's words are a walk down a mountain path. It feels to Teuku like there should be more letters, more words, as the path abruptly breaks to a steep drop. Across the gap must be more letters, but they are distant and blurry and Teuku longs for whatever thoughts there are on the other side, the thoughts Fred traps within his own skull.

***

In the past few days, the clouds have rolled themselves up into a thick wool sheet that grays out the sky. They are heavy now, hanging low enough that Mt. Kerinci's peak pierces through the blanket. There are distant growls, far away from the island. The rains are intermittent, drenching falls that soak the earth until the mud is soft and spongy beneath Teuku's feet. Each step slurps; he can't help but giggle because it sounds like passing gas. The water is perpetually draining into the cave where it has begun to sound like a running faucet at all times. He wants to tell Abbey of the otters in the deep cave, but Teuku knows the rhythm of the skies and he knows Abbey will not leave if she learns. The scientists are nearly done digging out the skull, but it is becoming dangerous to linger. The cave will soon flood. The heavier rains are coming.

When he warns Abbey, she is silent. Her eyes wander to Lucas who is hunched over the skull, using a knife-like tool to carve away the rock. It is still embedded in the earth. Where the right jaw bone meets the rest of the skull is submerged in dark stone. Abbey looks back down at Teuku, "We're almost done. We can do this before the rain."

She tries to move to the skull, but Teuku takes her wrist. "There will be more water than your team can handle. The trucks will sink. We will not make it back."

"We'll take our chances," she says, pulling away and joining Lucas.

***

In the morning, Teuku and Abbey sit side-by-side on a grounded log. His father is beneath a canvas tent to their left. They watch him drop a machete blade into the spiky hide of a durian he found wandering the woods with Fred. The warm pungency of the fruit inside bleeds into the air. Abbey wrinkles her nose; her throat coughs a disgusted groan. Teuku laughs. Abbey smiles and Teuku feels his cheeks warm the moment her teeth appear between her lips, white as salt. Teuku looks away, upward. He says, "Eat without breathing."

Above, the gray sky gently growls like a starved belly. Abbey asks, "Is the monsoon season bad?"

Teuku nods; his eyes do not leave the clouds. "The river floods some years."

"Explains why a young skull is buried in rock," she says.

"May I ask what it is about the otters?"

She hums affirmatively. "It's looking for something and having faith that it exists out there. That's what it's like searching for these endangered animals. They might not be on the planet anymore. If that's true, they won't be ever again. Just, poof, gone. Nothing but bones. But if we can find one here, if we can help it to survive, there's a chance. I hate the thought of something just disappearing like that."

"Do you fear death, Abbey? We see death every year. Bodies floating in the river. Bodies floating in the flood. Children starved. When a person goes away, she is gone. All thoughts and feelings, opinions, bad habits. The person is gone. It is only flesh. Have you ever seen a dead body, Abbey?" She doesn't answer and he continues. "I have. In my own village. Countless bodies. My mother among them."

"I'm so sorry."

"Do not be. The sky is clear above the clouds. The storm took away my mother. The storm did not last. The sun returned."

"And so will the storm."

"And so will mothers. All things return."

"I don't think that's true."

"Not in the same way. Your otter, if it is gone, will return. Maybe in another otter. Maybe another creature. Nature finds a way. All things return to balance."

"That's substitution. Something filling in a niche because something else is gone."

"No, it is faith in the world. Our faith and your faith are very different. But faith is always the same: it is the belief that a power or force, with or without intent, eventually makes things as they should be."

***

Teuku's father rounds the campfire and kneels beside his son. He says in Malaysian, "We should go tomorrow morning. We are not needed and the rains come soon."

"They do not know the danger of the rains, Father. We brought them here. We are responsible for ensuring their safety."

The ends of Teuku's father's thick black brows reach for one another, stretching into a scowl. He scolds, "You were not responsible for your mother."

Teuku nods slowly. His gaze pans leisurely to the skeletal tent, aglow like a great white Chinese lantern, Abbey's dark silhouette imposed into the fabric with such ferocity that black bleeds to the other side. There is a roar of men across the camp. Lucas's dark head and shoulders sprout up from a bundling of bodies. He dumps a bottle of beer down his throat, accompanied by a chorus of cheers. "Again!" chant the scientists. He does it again. And again. Laughter, applause, chants and roars drown out the song of Sumatra. Teuku can no longer hear the birds tweeting, nor the usually constant clicking of insects that reminds Teuku of the symphony of keystrokes inside the internet café he and his school friends spend their summers in.

His father places a palm on his shoulder. Teuku says without looking, "Maybe I was not responsible for Mother, but I am certainly responsible for these Americans."

***

The sky empties itself upon the site. It has been falling since morning, though a rush of interns dismantled the camp and departed with remarkable haste. Now the trucks are gone. There is only Teuku's father's car. It might be light enough to not fall into the mud, but Teuku doubts it. There is not long. His father paces around inside the dig site tapping his foot. They use flashlights again in the absence of the lamps. Abbey keeps saying, "We almost have it," as if her words might be magic, as if truth might shift to match them. Their tools are beginning to slip against the wet stone. The water is creeping from the deep cave, inching toward the clearing from the tunnel Teuku took days earlier. It is already half a centimeter deep in the clearing. Teuku thinks the flood will drown the skull before it can be freed. Still, he kneels beside Abbey, lets the rough edges of rocky floor cut into the flesh of his knees, and he hammers against the stone surrounding the skull.

From the tunnel to the cave's mouth, there is the sound like television static. It grows louder, then quiets, then grows again. Each time the volume swells, Teuku feels his heart race. The smell of mold has snaked through the paths from the inner cave and saturates the air with its musk. The way the flashlights bounce from the wet ground and how the water bows to their feet makes it look like they are all standing on a flimsy sheet of plastic.

Lucas says, "I don't know if we can keep this up."

"We have to," says Abbey. A bead of sweat drips off her nose. Great, Teuku thinks. More water.

Their tools are ineffective. The flooding brings in new mud and rocks from outside. Teuku is up to his ankles and his shoes are heavy. He hates having wet socks.

Lucas shouts, "We got the jaw bone!" He lifts it high. It looks like a staple made of ivory. A rush of sloshing water pours in from the exit. It's really coming now. Abbey is still crouched, her arms submerged to the elbows.

"That tells us nothing," she says. Desperation croaks her voice. "We have to see the brow. We need at least a picture of it."

Teuku's father starts yelling. "We go now! The river come. Tunnel short." He beckons with his hands.

He's right. Teuku forgot about the passage with the low ceiling. Waiting any longer might mean drowning on the way out. The river would eventually flood the cave. The force of the water outside would blast them deep into the cave's belly.

Lucas shouts, "Abbey, come on!"

"No, this is too important."

"We might have caught them on the camera traps too!"

She doesn't respond. Teuku's arm is grabbed. His father is dragging him out. Before he turns, he sees Lucas bend and hoist Abbey up. Her screams and pleas bounce in the cavern chamber. It is all Teuku can hear until he is squeezing through the tunnel crawl space and streams of monsoon rain clog up his ears and drain into his mouth and nostrils. It is too much water. It is too fast. He gags. It tastes like iron. He starts coughing. His father keeps pulling on him, then jerking forcibly. The water crushes against his chest, pushing him back down the hole. Everything is black. He can hear the roar of wind, a ghastly growl as huge volumes of air are thrown into the cave's mouth. They must be close. Teuku fights to keep his head above water, gasping greedily. He chokes on chunks of mud that wash into his throat. Then he feels his father yank once more.

And then he feels nothing but a punch of water blowing against his ribs. Teuku tumbles, collides with jagged rock. He rolls backward, unsure of up or down, left or right. His body slaps against something soft. Through a second of open eyes, he sees Lucas's dark silhouette clinging to a spike of stone. The sound of water intensifies. Teuku is thrown back down the tunnel again and Lucas is lost in the darkness.

The clearing has become a pool. Teuku cannot reach the ground, but the water is calmer here. He shouts for Abbey as he floats. There is no longer any light.

"Teuku! Where are you?"

So she too has fallen. Dread opens up inside Teuku's stomach. They will die here. Even the echoes pose problems—Teuku does not know what direction Abbey's voice came from. "I do not know," he gasps. Now he adds, "Do you feel the water pulling?" He can feel the water sucking at his legs; he does not think it should be doing this.

"No," she replies. "You must be near the tunnel to—Oh God, Teuku, that'll turn into a whirlpool. Swim away!"

He gargles again. It is too late. The water constricts around his body like a serpent and then he is sucked down, tumbling again through a narrow passage. The last thing he hears is Abbey's scream for him.

***

Teuku wakes to an orchestra of water: tonal drips, the tinkling streams draining down from the surface, gurgling bubbles as the air that had been stirred into the mud escape. It is dark and there is no difference between opening his eyes and closing. Insects make sounds like motors, percussive flapping that swells into a croaking moan. He feels something with many legs scurry over his stomach. A crab, he thinks.

A voice hovers above him in the darkness, softly chanting his name. He knows it is Abbey, but he cannot see her. Her hands touch his chest, pressing his damp t-shirt against his skin. The pain spreads like butter, radiating down to his abdomen. He groans and tries to curl up, but the movement rouses new aches to blare fanfares against his nerves. Everything hurts—his right shoulder, his left forearm, both knees, the left side of his shin, at least three points on his back and a throbbing sting above his right ear. Teuku blinks and feels the warm water of his tears run down his temples. Abbey cries, "Oh God, Teuku. Are you okay?"

He wants to speak, but the effort ignites his body into sudden agony; he moans again instead. And though it is already dark, Teuku recedes to a deeper darkness. He falls again, this time into the cave of his own skull.

***

He wakes to find himself bouncing to a staggered rhythm. Abbey's breaths are hoarse and labored. There is more light now, but just scarcely. Just enough to see the moisture of the cave glimmer like faint diamonds. Abbey is mid-sentence when Teuku comes to—something about her mother—and he realizes that she has strapped him to her back. He lets his ear rest against her back. Abbey ends every sentence with a question for Teuku. He tries to tell her that he is awake, but every step awakens each injury and it takes all Teuku has to suppress the pain. When he feels his shirt jostling against his chest from the movement, the way the fabric sticks to him and then tears away with a stinging heat, he realizes he is bleeding. He groans weakly, stirring against the straps binding his body to hers. Her voice changes, "Teuku! You're awake again! Don't go to sleep, okay? I think you have a concussion."

Teuku does not know what that word means, but his belly

bursts into burning when he tries to ask, so he just nods his head against her back.

"You're going to be okay," she says. "I'm not going to let us die here."

He does not tell her he is bleeding. He does not need to. He is sure she can feel the warmth of it soaking through her shirt.

***

"There might not be any exit," says Abbey. Teuku is now lying again on the cave floor. The mud has returned to rock and the roughness aggravates his lacerations. He can see the dim shadow of Abbey's figure squatting with her back leaned up against a stone. "We're as endangered as that damned otter."

Teuku manages a whisper, "No."

She crawls to him in haste. "Teuku? Are you okay? How are you feeling?"

"Hurt," he says. He tries to fake a chuckle, but the contraction of his stomach feels like being beat with a pipe.

"We need to keep moving, Teuku. Can you walk yet?"

He stirs. "Yes, I ca—ergh." He collapses.

"Come on," she says, laboring to her feet. She moves to him, turns and squats so he's presented with her back. Teuku drapes his arms over her shoulders. She begins to tie his forearms together and he realizes now that he has leather thongs on his wrists and a bungee cord is cinched around his waist. She takes the cord and wraps it around her hips so that his weight is dispersed and then she rises and continues the walk.

"Thank you," whispers Teuku.

"I'm not going to let you die down here."

Her pace quickens. It jars Teuku's injuries all the more and he falls silent for a moment to gather the strength to push the pain down. He is crying again. Does he fear death? If he had the strength, he would give Abbey a squeeze. She is the one who concerns him. He whispers, "These Americans, always thinking they can change the way of things. Eventually, we too shall pass and the world will heal from our actions. All things are nature, even us. What we take away will be returned."

"Sounds like a good reason to not even try."

"I did not say that."

"What are you even saying? How much blood have you lost, Teuku? Are you feeling okay? Concussed people spout nonsense, you know."

"I am saying," he begins, but it is slow. He needs more rest. His throat feels rough, like the tissue inside resembles dried sponge. He needs water. Abbey must need even more. He forces the last words before his mind falls again inside himself: "that we are the clouds."

***

There is a tunnel in Mt. Kerinci that begins one thousand meters up and slithers through the mountain down to sea level. It formed over millions of years when a large pond on the mountain's side collected enough moisture to begin dripping into the stone, eroding the rock little by little. The streams of water formed a vast subterranean network of highways that all converged on the ground. This point birthed the river that, for millennia, was home to the hairy-nosed otters before the colonies of hairless apes spread so vast and consumed so much that, little by little, the creatures dwindled in their numbers. And then the numbers themselves became phantoms. And the creatures themselves became myths. And the earth only kept a record in bones.

It is on the mountain by the pond that Abbey emerges from a cavern mouth, a lifeless boy strapped to her back. She collapses to the dirt, cries hot and angry tears, pounds small knots of fists into the soft earth. She lays the boy down and the mud yields to his body such that he is depressed into it. Such that the browns of his skin and the rich soft soil blur together. Such that from above, one can only see this pale woman, blotched with brown mud and blood, bowing down into the earth.

She does not yet realize how far she has climbed, how many hours were spent in the dark tunnel, nor where precisely upon Mt. Kerinci this clearing rests. She does not yet realize that in eras past, when the earth was still an embryo, fissures below the surface collided, sprouting a spire of stone to the skies. Each subterranean boom caused the dagger of rock to stab higher and higher, but one collision in particular quaked with such force that the stone was severed. Boulders cascaded in an avalanche. The slice of mountain rolled back to ground level and eventually was beat into soil and dirt and pebbles by waters from the skies. This ancient moment in planetary incubation carved the flatness that would become the pond that would create the tunnel that would hollow out the cave that would form the river that would house the otters. This cutting of the stone saved her life.

She does not yet realize how the sun beats upon her back. She does not yet notice how cool the air is, how shallow her breaths must be to gather the necessary gases to sustain her tissues. She does not yet realize that she must travel through the heavy, low blanket of storm clouds to reach her team. Nor that below, the monsoon still drenches the island, the river still threatens to flood. Nor that the only clouds above her are thin, light ribbons of pulled cotton.

She only sees the body of the boy, the mud crabs that crawl upon his belly, the memories of the dark tunnel and the precise moment she realized she could no longer feel his chest inflating with life against her back.

And because of this, she does not notice the colony of otters watching her curiously from the far edge of the pond, the otters that have made this their last refuge, up high above the clouds. They drift through the water and, with slow apprehension, approach the strange creature kneeling in the mud. They gather silently behind her as she weeps. They sit and watch. Then a mud crab upon the boy begins to move and one otter perks his nose up.

He does not dash to claim the meal. He hesitates. His brothers and his sisters turn around. There are mud crabs elsewhere. As Abbey takes her knife and cuts the cords that tether her to Teuku, the otters retreat. A sound slithers up the slope of Mt. Kerinci from below. It is a groan of thunder from the monsoon clouds that wrap around the mountain just meters beneath her. She decides she must rise, must wash away the earth and blood from her skin in the waters of the pond. When she turns around, there is only a crab dragging itself through the mud. The otters are already gone.

The Message of My Skin

I can already see what Mr. Jordan meant on the phone when he said this was urgent—the pod of four squid in the tank float still with the spears of their heads all pointing to the left, one eye fixed to the cuttlefish tank across from them. In concert, a hint of yellow bleeds over their chalk-white skin until they are thickly painted with it. They flash brilliantly twice and then the color collapses suddenly. They are white again. The process repeats. This has never happened before; they look hypnotized.

As I approach, I notice the cuttlefish mimicking with a red-brown shade over yellow. They shouldn't be able to see each other through the glass. Still, it looks like a conversation.

Dr. Amendola says, "I'm stumped."

Mr. Jordan responds to her, "Well, we ought to go over what was happening before this started." Now he looks at me and his round cheeks pull up into golf balls as he smiles. "Doctor! So glad you could make it in. What do you reckon?"

I shrug. "A reaction to some sort of electromagnetic field from the machinery?"

"Maybe," says Mr. Jordan. "You two are the smart folks. That's why I pay you. Figure it out."

His laughter is a mechanical cackle, loud and percussive and stuttering. Dr. Amendola's eyes do a slow pull toward me, one side of her lips stretches toward her ear in a line. I shrug again. Mr. Jordan squeezes his body between me and the squid tank as he moves for the door, dragging the laugh along with him.

He's an odd sort of man, a forty-something balding Wall

Street type who sits on the board for three different competing technology companies. The rich are always a little insane. Mr. Jordan keeps his hair—what's left of it looks like a half-eaten dough-nut ring—in frayed brown spires, tufts that emerge chaotically like a mountain range. I think he's just trying to look crazy, but when he hired me, he told me how he went whale-watching in Alaska with his wife four years ago and the aurora borealis was talking to him in code.

He's been recruiting a team of specialists for the SETI Insti-tute, an experimental initiative going beyond the traditional search for radio waves. He wants to look for light, some message coded into photons streaking through space. Mr. Jordan procured this small lab—really just a room with the two tanks, a wall of TV monitors, and another wall that has a table pressed up against it, all manner of papers scattered over the surface.

I'm a linguist. I've been studying the squid to see how they communicate through color. I'm looking for patterns, trying to figure out how the squid know that a sequence of small dots means *crab* and pink means *cuttlefish* or that the series of blue-purple-teal-purple-red are instructions on where a food source is. It's a laborious process; humans aren't designed to understand light as a language. If I'm successful, I'll become a legend. They'll call me the forefather of photolinguistics; I'll be immortal. Every linguist for the rest of time will know the name Tom When.

"I'm going home," says Dr. Amendola. "You don't need to stay."

I reply, "I'm already here. Might as well." There's always more work to do.

"Suit yourself," she says, and then retraces Mr. Jordan's path out.

Now I am alone with the floating brains, gazing through the glass. We film every second of their day. We know that the males turn white when proposing a sexual encounter. They wear black stripes to signal aggression toward other squid. The threat of another species is coded with a series of bright and abrupt flashes through the yellow-green spectrum. We also understand many of their hunting signals. There are different patterns of communica-tion depending on rank, and it certainly looks like one squid in particular is calling the shots. I've been calling him General Cthulhu. It normally gets some laughs.

If this pattern weren't so abnormal, my guess would be that they're trying to proposition the cuttlefish to some inter-species mating. It does seem like a mixture of the two. There is something off about it though, something that lures my curiosity. It feels like a yarn unspooling inside me, its thread slurped up by the squid. And now I notice General Cthulhu isn't performing the same sequence as the others. He has a sliver of pink on his side, a small worm of color that dances along the surface of his flesh, curling and uncurling, folding up, stretching out, collapsing into a single dot, and then becoming a string slithering to his eye. He resembles a lava lamp, fluorescent globs gliding beneath glass skin.

My phone buzzes in my pocket.

Conner's voice trawls through the phone line, a little jerky and hesitant. "Hey, Tam, *em trai dai! Toi can mot dac an.* What're you doing?"

Confession: I was not born Tom When; I was born Tam Nguyen. I am Vietnamese. When they write my biography, I hope they leave this bit out. My work should be more important than the shape of my eyes. And let's be honest—the Vietnamese are awful people.

Conner's my brother, born Cung. He's one of the few people who calls me Tam still. I say, "I'm at work. Something strange happened. Strange colors."

"What does that mean?" he asks.

"Hell if I know."

"Sorry."

I start tapping my foot, waiting for whatever it is that Conner needs me for this time. The sound of my sole clicking on the tile is swallowed up by slurping water filters. "What's the problem?"

"We should talk tonight."

I sigh. I tell him, "I don't have time for this, Conner."

"No, no, it's an emergency," he says. "I really need your help."

"Fine. When and where?"

***

When we were younger, Conner was bullied a lot. In second grade, there was a fat white boy named Louie Puller who called Conner *Cunt*. This was back when we still went by Tam and Cung. I was in the third grade, but we shared the same recess hour. I used to climb on top of the monkey bars, balance my thighs across one of the thick sides, and let my legs dangle like draped ropes. I liked the high perch, being able to see all the other kids run around, playing basketball or tag; I watched the swing sets make pendulums of the girls, their bodies arcing through the air. I could also watch Conner, who often found a quiet corner in the shade where he and his friends could play a card game. It was a private place, away from the eyes of the teachers, away from where most of the popular and athletic kids played.

There was a day when Louie and his tiny posse—a taller white boy named George and a skinny black boy named Davon—walked across the black top toward Conner. Louie had a red dodge ball under his arm. George and Davon kept passing glances and cackles to one another. There was a fierce determination painted on Louie's face that reddened his round cheeks enough that his freckles melted away.

And then the ball launched. It smacked into Conner's face, bowled him over onto his butt. The sidekicks rolled into laughter; Louie waddled closer. I leapt from my perch and ran to my brother just in time to hear Louie spit, "My dad tells me you chinks killed his best friend." The fat boy threw his shoe square into Conner's stomach. My brother curled up like a shrimp on the ground. Louie said, "My dad is… because of you, Cunt. You don't belong here." His voice cracked in the middle and his eyes went wet.

Louie swung another kick. The kids had encircled the fight. The teachers were around the corner, watching the others play basketball. Conner's playing spot was too hidden, too private.

I leapt at Louie, latched my limbs to his. His legs collapsed when I kicked out the backs of his knees. I dragged the lard-ball to the ground, belly down, and then I straddled the small of his back like I was riding a whale. My fingers clutched a knot of his hair, yanked up his skull, threw it back down into the pavement. The other kids must have cringed when they heard the soft sound of his skin splitting on the cement, a squish and a rip. The second smack was harder, more percussive, a thwack like a coconut breaking open. I was meditative in my assault. He tried pressing up from his hands and I squeezed my knees into the folds of his fat, forced his head down again.

Louie was limp beneath me, but it didn't matter. I couldn't stop. I tightened my clutch on his scalp. I lifted myself up, led him by the hairs to roll onto his back, looked at his lacerated face, his mangled mouth, the lumps of red and purple his eyes had become. And I made stones of my fists. And I hammered his head until the sharp bones of his teeth split the skin of my knuckles. And no one could tell anymore whether the red splatters upon the sidewalk were mine or his.

***

When I get to Conner's door and he lets me in, he pokes his head out and throws it left and right first. And then he rushes me inside, shuts the door with force, locks and deadbolts it hastily. He's sweating. There are dark patches on the underarms of his t-shirt. The whole place is dark and barren. There's only the light that bleeds in from the kitchen. We sit on the couch. There are no remotes or magazines on his coffee table, just a silver ashtray containing three crushed cigarette butts. He tangles his fingers together in his lap and is bouncing both legs to alternate rhythms. His eyes dart around in his skull with erratic jerks.

I ask, "So what is it?"

He pauses for a moment with his eyes trained to the ground. The memory of beating Louie invades my mind. Something in my stomach thrashes wildly; I try to justify the assault every year, telling myself I was protecting Conner, but I always feel relief that Conner doesn't like to look me in the eye. When he lifts his head up to me, I turn my eyes away. Conner exclaims, "Oh!" and gets to his feet and runs behind the kitchen counter, digging frantically through a drawer, chanting, "Where is it? Where is it?"

Now Conner looks up. His face is red, greasy; his hair too, like he hasn't showered in days. There's a wet black mop sprouting from his head. I ask again, "What is it this time?"

"I'm in trouble, man. Real trouble," he says. This doesn't surprise me. Conner asks, "Do you remember Duc?"

Duc is one of the ring-leaders at Eden, the Vietnamese

neighborhood; he's short and bald and normally hangs at the bil-
liards hall I-Cue. The guy has tattoo sleeves wrapping up both arms
and a mythological sort of build—like a demi-god—where his del-
toids are as huge and round as his head. I don't answer Conner.
Duc is hard to forget. The last time I saw him, he got in a fist fight
with this college guy because the kid lost a bet he had no money
for. The kid was in the hospital for two days.

Conner starts explaining. His words come galloping out:
"Okay, okay, so I owe Duc some money and it's really late and I
need to borrow."

"How much?"

"A couple grand."

"Out of the question."

"You know I'm good for it!"

He isn't. No matter how good Conner is at pool, giving
him money is like throwing the bills into a shredder. But he's family and I'm responsible for him.

"Okay, okay," he says. "Could you at least give this five
hundred to him?" Conner hands me a wad of Franklins.

"You can't?" I ask.

"I don't want him asking about the rest. Seriously, he might
hurt me. Come on, you're family."

"Fine," I say.

***

Now General Cthulhu is a pinkish orange shade. He floats
just above the bottom of the tank while the others lazily drift in
circles above the large oval balloon of his head. His tentacles fray
out in curls that make me think of a handle-bar moustache. Other
colors—red like fresh blood, sea salt green, dark violet like a cow's
tongue—ebb into and out of his skin. I am alone again in the
lab; Dr. Amendola has been in her office down the hall typing up
another report. Cthulhu's light bleeds across the screen of glass,
tinting the window, luring all of my attention.

I can feel it trickle through my neurons like centipedes,
millions of their tiny legs pricking across the surface of my brain.
Something shifts. My body lurches forward, weight falling to the
balls of my feet, nose closing in toward the glass, spilling a kaleido-

scopic film over my face. My fingertips touch the wall of the tank; it's warmer than I expect.

General Cthulhu is a strobe light of Easter colors—pink, orange, green, and blue. The rhythm is fast, urgent. It has to be a message, but he pays no mind to the other squid.

In the reflection of the glass, I see a white star—the cuttlefish are beaming brightly in the tank behind me. I turn around. There are three in that tank, flat disks floating and flashing like flying saucers in the sky. They are a chorus of photons. I step out of the way and try to watch both. Mr. Jordan must be right. This looks like an argument.

And then the cuttlefish suddenly stop. They drift aimlessly. Cthulhu sails to the corner of his tank nearest to me. The hairs on my body become erect like the quills of a porcupine.

Cthulhu floats and flashes; he turns the fat spear of his body so that he can stare one of his beady eyes at me. His tentacles go still and I get the feeling he wants me to say something. He keeps watching me as if expecting me to change color. I stay yellow. I am only yellow, and he eventually turns his attention away to something else. For the next few days, he ignores me entirely like I am just part of his scenery. He treats me like I'm the one that cannot speak.

***

It is winter. Before the sun fully sets, a silvered sky speaks to us in sleet; a sheet of snow and rain and ice slicken the streets. I drag a cigarette outside of I-Cue, push a piston of smoke into the air. I try to gather up all the courage I can to step inside. My boot snuffs out the dropped butt before I turn and pass through the doors.

I-Cue is in a strip mall called the Eden Center twenty minutes outside of Washington, D.C. It's the Vietnamese sanctuary for the East Coast. They hung a South Vietnamese flag on a pole, saluted a nation that no longer was, spoke their native tongue, and shunned the whites and the blacks and the browns. But originally, Eden was only a tangent. A few miles east was Clarendon, the first neighborhood the Vietnamese settled into.

My father made this his home. He was seventeen when he

left Vietnam, already too old to grasp new words with ease. Because my grandfather had been a physics professor and now unloaded trucks, my father went from a privileged class to the lowest class. He was yellow in a white world and all the speech around him stuttered and stammered out. The language had no music to him. Sentences only curled up when asking questions. How could they tell one word from the next without singing it? It was all a drone to him, boring and lifeless.

Immigrants to America all seek power and wealth in different ways. When the Chinese came to this country, they worked the railroads. When the Vietnamese came, we worked the cocaine trade. It was an easy in for power when language and education sought to oppress us. My father became a driver—sixteen hours south to Florida and then back, five hundred grand of white bricks concealed in the cavities of his car doors. A mechanic in Clarendon would remove the frames to extract the product.

The entrance to *I-Cue* is a deep staircase and another door. Past the door is darkness, dim lamps suspended above green tables. A littering of ethnic bodies populates the floor space. They wear ratty t-shirts splotched with coffee stains or tank tops torn at the shoulder. Their skin is brown or gold or copper, yellow hues that are amplified in the lamp light. The choir of colliding balls creates a staccato drumming I feel beating against my heart; it tenses my muscles, pulls my shoulders back, readies my hands to lash out into battle. I map in my mind the geography of a battle, whose skull I can smash into what, where to leap next. No one even looks at me though.

There is a door at the far corner that leads into the kitchen. A hidden staircase there descends into the dungeon. Entry is password-protected. They hold cock fights there. The losers are turned into chicken pho; the hormones of their rage produce a stronger soup. The chamber is also home to one of seven cocaine operations—the one that Conner works for.

I am relieved to see Duc at a billiard table. The thought of going deeper, of entering their underworld, twists me up. I'm already nauseated. We make eye contact; his is a glaring sort, nose down to the globes scattering beneath him, pupils half-hidden under the menace of his brow. He pumps a subtle and sinister nod. I approach.

"Tam," he says without a smile. *"Toi khong co thay may nhieu nam."*

I say, "Conner has something for you."

"Het tien roi." He grins. *"Choi khong?"*

I shake my head and say, "You know I don't play." I hand him the wad of bills and he counts it in the open.

Now his eyes ignite and I see his knuckles go white around the cue stick. *"Troi dat! Cung het tien, ha? May de lua toi?"* He's spitting curses, demanding to know if I'm trying to cheat him.

The end of his stick is at my throat. He snarls and I am still. He speaks through gritted teeth, *"Anh noi Cung, dem tao tien het. Khong co tien het, tao giet Cung."* Tell Cung to bring me all the money, or I'll kill him.

***

I have heard nothing from Conner for a week. I imagine he is off on another run. When our father did his runs, he was gone for two weeks at a time. Our mother fixed meals of rice and *cha lua*—a gray cold sausage textured like rubber—night after night until he returned, a smile smeared on his face such that his moustache curled up beneath his nose and then hung off the corners of his lips. For a few months, our wealth was restored. And then it was depleted and he departed again. There is always some anxiety when Conner is gone; I always have to wonder if he'll be lost like our father.

After a particularly long day at the lab, Dr. Amendola asks if I want to go for a drink. We head to a place in the Clarendon neighborhood of Arlington. In the 90s, a large gentrification effort shepherded the Vietnamese community toward Eden. It happened in an instant: one day, you just noticed how all the eyes that once seemed pressed so harshly at the edges suddenly popped into great round circles. The Hunan, a clinging vestige from the old Clarendon, operates as a typical Chinese restaurant during the day. After six each night, it becomes a bar that the young, the rich, and the white flock to in order to feel more cultured because they are taking sake bombs.

The lights dim. Neon cords that slither invisibly along the ceiling burst into electric pinks and blues and greens. The left wall stacks fish tanks like tiles—during the day, they house lobsters, trout, bass, squid and octopus, compacted clusters of crabs, schools of shrimp and snails. At five, the staff wheels over holding tanks and ferries these creatures to the back. Tropical sea creatures invade the tanks: a crowd of clown fish, electric blue regal tang, thousands of those tiny bioluminescent cleaner fish with the glowing laser stripes on their sides, blowfish that're richly red. Each tile is backlit by black light such that each creature's fluorescence leaps violently off the glass.

The acoustics of the restaurant shift from the winding pitch bends of classical Chinese into the blasts of bass of Top 40s hits, cranked until the music drowns out any conversations below a bellow.

Dr. Amendola and I sit at the bar, facing one another in our stools. I have an elbow propped on the bar top; the aquarium wall is in my view over her shoulder, revealing a dragon fish floating lonesome in its own tank. Its body is serpentine, shaped like a tilde with frayed protrusions along its length. The shade of its orange scales looks like plasma flowing along its body in waves. Dr. Amendola sips her vodka-cranberry; her lips and drink are the same shade of pink. I ask, "Why cephalopods?"

She smiles and says, "Because studying them is like studying every science at once. Neuroscience—you know, the brain thing—and linguistics and biology and chemistry. It's just remarkable. Did you know many of them can shapeshift? Their bodies are so malleable that they can make any shape they want, change the density of their bodies, change the texture of their skin. Some can literally turn invisible; some can perfectly mimic other creatures."

"You don't say." I sip my whisky.

She touches my arm. "Yes! These are creatures that can shapeshift, who have higher-order cognition, who have language! If there's an alien species out there, if they're anything like cephalopods, then we're going to be doomed."

She is grinning when she says all of this. I have an eye on the dragon fish. It's turned to look at me. I wonder if it can see through the glass. The cadence of our conversation stutters to a stop. Then she asks, "So is *When* Chinese? Korean?"

This is something a white person always asks eventually: *So what kind of Asian are you? Oh, I love pho. I eat it every weekend. I answer,* "That sounds about right." *I think about saying, And you?*

What kind of white are you? Italian? I love pizza.
"Chinese? Do you speak any?"
"Not in the slightest." Now I laugh. I tell her, "I can't speak my native language anymore. Isn't that crazy?"
"Really?" She asks. "That is! Especially since you're a linguist."
The bartender—a thin Asian with spiked hair—leans over the bar and points at my empty glass. "Tam," he says, "*muon uong mot nua, khong?*"
I blink twice, look at the bartender. The same Vietnamese-speaking Chinese family still owns the Hunan, but I can't tell if I recognize him. I say, "Beg your pardon?"
He chuckles. It doesn't seem sinister, but I get a chill. He repeats, still in Vietnamese. Now he points at my empty glass. I nod. Dr. Amendola touches my hand again when the bartender turns away to refill me. She asks, "Do you get that a lot? People speaking Chinese to you?"
I laugh. It's probably too nervous, too broken up and stuttering. "Yeah," I say. "I think he thought I was someone else." I turn over my shoulder to look at the bartender. He slides my drink across the bar to me with an unblinking glare. He prints off a new receipt with the updated order, streaks a ribbon over the total with a highlighter and slips it in front of us. I look at the stripe of yellow on the receipt, the way it seems to leap off the white under the black light. I get the feeling that the bartender is calling me a fraud.

***

I am not sure when I return to Eden, but I am inside *I-Cue* walking into the kitchen. The deep fryers hiss and sizzle, a menacing sound as they crisp the skins on shoe-string potatoes and chicken wings. One of the cooks—a skinny guy with a goatee and long hair tied back into a ponytail—nods at me. I keep a flat face, make myself look as tough as I can manage, furrow a brow, and return a stiff nod his way. The secret door is a shelf of condiments. I slide bottles of hoisin and sriracha out of the way, rap a knuckle against the wall to the rhythm of South Vietnam's ancient national anthem, and then I wait.
A corded black phone hangs on the wall beside the shelf. It

rings. I answer.

The voice on the other end is an older man, his throat tuned to a higher register. He asks rudely, "*Ai do?*"

I respond, "*Chao, Bac. Nguyen Tam day. Anh cua Nguyen Cung.*" The Vietnamese feels like phlegm fixed to my throat.

I can hear him laughing at my American accent. He says, "Ah! Nguyen Tam! *Chao, chao. Cho mot chut. Bac di len, okay?*"

The *okay* is jarring, a forced monotone of bad English. I repeat it and hang up the phone, wait for him to come up and open the door.

I can hear Bac Sieu on the other side of the shelf, all the various locks rattling, clicking, sliding out of place. Next, the shelf inches forward, away from the wall, and then slides to the side. Bac Sieu is revealed in the secret staircase, a withered wrinkled man smiling through a snaggletooth. He used to work at Dat Hung, a jewelry store in Clarendon my father used to frequent so he could play *tien len*—the Vietnamese national card game—in the backroom.

We descend the stairs. Bac Sieu pats my back, tells me how long it's been since he's seen me, asks how my father is doing and how many years of his sentence are left. I answer truthfully—I don't know. We step out of the stairs and into the main room. Dim light bulbs hang naked from the ceiling. There are six tables peopled; they are playing cards, wrinkled bills at their center. Bac Sieu faces me so I have to linger with him. He tells me of the seventies, of him and my father as young men discovering America for the first time, of what a relief it was to be in a land free from rifles and falling bombs, of their exhilaration with the limitless potential they felt. And then his voice croaks something sullen and the wrinkles of his face, once curled with his grinning, fall flat into rows. "America is not all that it promised," he says. "America demands assimilation."

This basement chokes on the smog of cigarettes. It obscures the light, smears out the details of every face. Still, I can recognize Duc where he's seated, the width of his shoulders, the confidence with which he leans upon the table, weighing it down with his whole body through his forearms. He sees me too, a casual glance through the silver screen of smoke. I shake Bac Sieu's hand, thank him and approach Duc's table.

The other three men look for a moment, but return their

attention to their cards. Duc grins, holds a pausing hand to the three, and says to me, "*Chao, Tam! Nhieu nam Anh xuong day, ha? Co tien cua tao, khong?*"

I shake my head and move in so I am standing over Duc, looking down on him. "Khong. I don't have the money."

"*Anh biet tao giet em anh?*" Duc doesn't lose his grin. He owns this part of the world.

I hook my foot on the front leg of his chair and then drive my knee up hard. Duc and the chair begin to topple backward. I slam my raised foot into his sternum, stapling him to the ground. The other men back away, watch cautiously. Everyone is watching now.

I press my weight into Duc. He is glaring at me, his hands grasping my ankle, trying to lift me and relieve the pressure. I grin and I think of Cthulhu because Duc's face is turning purple. He can't breathe with me weighing down his lungs like this. I whisper with as much menace as I can muster, "If you touch Conner, I will cut you up. I will peel the skin from your face. Do you understand? *Tao se giai phau may. Tao se lot vo mat cua may.*"

Duc is gasping, wheezing for air. I press my foot down harder. I ask again, "Do you understand me? Or has my accent gotten too thick?"

His eyes begin rolling back into his skull. He struggles to stay conscious. I ease up just enough for him to suck in a wheeze of air and then I press down again. The color in his face drains to red and then begins to purple once more. I smile down at him, taunting, "You see, Duc, I don't need to feel powerful. I already am. All I need is an excuse to experience the joy of destroying someone. If I'm going to be honest, Duc, part of me wants to see you try me. We can see how tough you really are."

I turn away, walk back up the stairs. No one moves, but their jaws hang loose and I see their eyes follow me as I turn to leave.

Sometimes, there is no doubt in my mind: I am the worst of them all. When I get home that night, I cry.

***

Dr. Amendola and I are poring over some new photographs. She thinks we're getting close, but I keep getting distracted. I wonder if I've accidentally doomed Conner to his death. I wonder if

Duc has the sense to fear me.

She asks, "What do you make of the purple and yellow pulses?"

We have been studying the pulses for weeks now. It is not an active communication and the squid and cuttlefish pulse at different rhythms, never synchronized. Dr. Amendola puts three film strips in front of me, one of the squid and two of the cuttlefish. Our notes describe each occasion of these patterns enduring for around forty minutes, no activity before or after. I walk over to the desk and lean over the keyboard and mouse. One of the televisions now displays two graphs, multi-colored spirals. I say, "These are the yellow-purple pulses for each species in the past month, charted by frequency. You'll notice that the squid's frequency is slowing over the month and the cuttlefish's is speeding."

"You think they're synchronizing?" she asks.

"No. They're transferring. Morphemes. Sets of grammatical rules. This is one way language evolves. It's like the syntax of the squid is being imposed onto the cuttlefish. Like one language is colonizing the other." What bothers me is that I think they are talking about me, talking about the mute yellow psychopath trying to eavesdrop on their private conversation.

***

Conner blasts through my front door that night. His voice booms with terror, "What the flying fuck, Tam!"

I am on my couch. The television is on and now I am staring open-mouthed at my brother standing at my door, face reddened like raspberries and eyes glaring through tears. He throws the door shut behind him, stares at me with a knot of disgust twisting his face, and then turns away, gripping a fistful of his hair. He shouts, "Jesus Christ, Tam, are you trying to get me killed?"

I stand. I say as calmly as I can, "I am trying to protect you."

"Yeah, protect me," he says. He turns again, stares me down. I can feel the fear radiating from him, like a slow creeping ooze of molten lava blistering out from his skin. Conner slams an open palm into my sternum. I tumble backward, twist my hips so I fall to the couch.

When I stand back up, Conner strides forward until we are nose to nose. He croaks an anguished cry and swings a fist.

Then another. The first strikes my jaw. The pain blooms on the surface of my cheek before soaking deeply and settling into my skull. I grit my teeth and parry the second with the blade of my forearm. Now I launch forward. Color floods my vision. I make a vise of my hand, snap it closed over Conner's throat. He spits out a gasp. I throw my knuckles into his face. A menaced whisper slithers through my teeth. "Do you have any idea what I can do to you?"

My grip tightens. His face is violet. Desperation is leaving his eyes. Everything is leaving his eyes. They are rolling up, losing focus on me or anything else. I release and his body folds up on the floor with a thud.

My face is hidden in my hands. I can see myself from the outside. I am hovering over this scene. I think, this is our nature. This is a helpless pattern. But the guilt opens over and over, a garden of rosebuds blooming one by one into fists of hot red coals. The blood drains from Conner's face.

In the seconds it takes for him to regain consciousness, my mind is buried under thoughts falling like an avalanche. I focus on the throbbing in my face, its heat and the pain that pulses with my heart.

Conner stirs, rolls onto his stomach, pushes himself up to a knee. I hoist him up and ask if he's okay. He throws me off him and leers.

I say, "I will pay Duc the rest. And then we leave that world, okay, Conner? We can end this forever. We don't need to be like them."

My brother's eye is black. His lip is cut. He holds a hand over his mouth and his skin is now wet and red and reflecting light back at me. I look at my own hands. My knuckles are not white anymore. My left hand is yellow again. My right hand is swelling, fat and purple. I might have broken a metatarsal.

Conner mutters, "It's like you're fucking bipolar."

I don't look up. I say, "I know. I should see a doctor." I burp up a brief chuckle. "I'm not right in the head, am I?" He's already gone.

I clean up in the bathroom. I stare at myself in the mirror. The left side of my face, throbbing with heat, is swollen round. There are so many shapes and colors on my cheek: a knot of black surrounded by a violet blossom encased in a ring of blue and then of green before slowly fading back to yellow. I stare into the glass for so long that my vision blurs. I can no longer make out the patterns. There is nothing there for me to read.

Flying Objects

It's the day after Nora confessed about her affair. She is in the bedroom when I arrive home from work. She's bent over, digging into the drawers of the dresser. I wonder if she's changing or packing. I don't think I want to know, but I'm sucked into the doorway. She's still dressed for work: purple blouse, a tight gray pencil skirt. My stomach stirs from the noxious image of her riding another man raw.

I gasp against the thought and Nora turns and faces me. She pulls her glasses off her face and sets them on the dresser top. She's always hated them; she thinks the frame's symmetry accentuates an awkward geometry in her face, like her bones have been set crooked.

Nora was a woman who'd had to grow into her beauty. It was obvious in her posture, the way she slacked her shoulders, the way she hung her head, hiding her face behind a curtain of hair. She'd paid for her good looks: teasings in childhood, humiliations in high school, invisibility in college. Even now, she's uncomfortable under a man's gaze, as if in fear that at any moment, he could turn on her. She shifts against the intrusive touch of my eyes.

Nora chews her lower lip.

"The dean assigned me to the excavation team for the wreckage in Lake Superior," I say.

"Oh," she says. "That sounds nice."

"They think it might be Felix Moncla's jet." This is my attempt at explaining why the team needs a historian.

"The alien guy?" asks Nora.

"Yeah, the alien guy."

Ste.-Sault Marie, Michigan—called "the Soo" by locals—is famous in UFO circles. Felix Moncla was an Air Force pilot who chased after a mysterious radar blip outside the city in 1953. The story goes that air traffic control detected an unidentified bogey on radar and sent Moncla out to intercept. Air traffic control watched the two radar blips when radio contact with Moncla was lost. And then the blips converged into one. When the screen refreshed, Moncla's aircraft and the bogey should have separated if they'd been at different altitudes. But it was black. Just black. The dots were gone. Felix Moncla was gone. They never found him, his jet, or the bogey he was intercepting. It's our city's biggest mystery: how does an entire fighter jet disappear?

"I hope it's a good experience for you," says Nora.

Now I notice her open luggage on the bed. She averts her eyes. I want to drag her down into an argument, dig up all the answers from inside her. But I can see guilt tugging at the muscles of her face.

When she leaves and the house empties, I realize I haven't turned the lights on. The living room is aglow in the optic blue of the television. An oppression sinks into me. All the dark spaces of our home fill up with Nora's absence. I am suddenly a stranger in my own home. There are new sounds: in the kitchen beside the living room, the blades of the kitchen ceiling fan slicing air, rhythmic like a metronome; the clocks of each room ticking and tocking, converging into a chorus of clattering clicks; the soles of my bare feet stripping from the hardwood floor with this sticky sort of sound. All this percussion, louder and clearer in her absence. There are sounds missing too: any of *The Doors*' albums Nora plays while she fixes dinner; her voice plunging into a mock baritone as she sings along with Jim Morrison crooning, *Come on, baby, light my fire*; the melody of her fixing dinner, whether a sizzle or a bubble or the drumming of wooden spoons against skillets.

I microwave my supper tonight. I eat in the dark. I dissect last night's dinner, reliving the moments. I need to figure out how this happened. We are across from each other on the small round table. We are in pajamas. Dinner is chicken, rice, an array of red, green and yellow peppers. We eat without speaking. I am comfortable. Then Nora sighs, straightens, her fork falls to her plate with a clink. Her eyes are wet. I ask, "What's wrong?"

Our gaze breaks. She is looking at her fork. "I met some-one. I mean, I *met* someone, Victor."

"What? What do you mean?" Her eyebrows are drawn up in the center, like she is begging with her eyes for forgiveness. And then her guilt is gone, transformed into impatience or anger. I can't tell which. "You've been having an affair? How? Why?"

"A coworker," says Nora. "It was just some drinks after work. But then he made me feel something I haven't in a long time. I don't know where it's going."

I become silent. Questions bombard my mind and yet not a single one escapes. Time creeps along. Nora stands, carries her plate to the sink and scrapes her dinner down the disposal. "For Christ's sake, Victor," she mutters. "Aren't you going to say some-thing?"

Terror tears a hole in my chest. If I say nothing, she'll leave. I force words from my gut; it feels like bile coming up. "What do you want from me?"

She throws her plate harshly into the sink. "I want you to want something!" She is gone from the kitchen. There's thunder from her steps storming up the stairs, and then there's the slam of our bedroom door. I can feel her wanting me to follow after, a violent tugging inside my head beckoning me to climb the stairs. I am too scared to move. I think maybe it's too late now. I think she doesn't care if it's too late; I know I just need to prove myself. I know that if I just show up in that doorway, it'll show to her that I care enough to try.

When I will my legs to move, nothing happens. My mind floods with all the things I could do wrong up there, all the things I've done wrong that threw her into another man's arms. I think about all the ways that I am not a man—how thin I am, how short, how meek. I can see myself running up there, my stomach swelling with a speech that sticks in my throat when I try to speak. Either the paradigm of silence pervades or the night expands with our fighting and at some point she will say something truly hurtful and I will clam up again and be right here anyway, legs folded over a cushion in the dark, head bowed down, wondering what at all I could possibly do to make this better.

I am on the couch for fifteen minutes sorting through these

visions. I want to stand up. There is stasis. I fall asleep on the couch.

***

The boat that we're using to get to the excavation site is a lot bigger than I expect it to be. I learn later that it's called a cabin cruiser. The seams of the boat are thin red lines of rust. Some of the floorboards on the deck are warped into valleys, sloping craters green with algae from pooled lake water. The boat smells of rotting eggs. A young man and woman are squeezing into wetsuits, checking the gauges on their equipment, nodding their heads as another man rattles off a list of instructions. He karate-chops both hands through the air as he talks; it's clear that he's the authoritative figure here. He's tall and broad. He has a strong face, a pronounced brow. He is the image of a primal man and I find it difficult to not hate him for it. I measure from every angle his superiority over me: his forearms are bowling pins and mine are rolling pins; his chest spreads open and mine collapses; his jaw is a lantern and mine a matchstick; his hair is cropped short, thick and full like fields of wheat before harvest, and mine is longer, messy, like a ball of alfalfa sprouts was thrown on my head. He becomes a container for my jealousy, even though Nora has always preferred mousier looking men. I lock my animosity up inside him so that it feels a moon's distance away. He explains to the divers how to operate the underwater camera; I recognize his voice from the phone. That's Roy, the lead investigator.

He glances at me. His eyes fall to the badge hanging off my neck, and then he smiles and offers an open hand. He's a disgustingly beautiful man when he smiles. I choke back the jealous urge to paste his face to my mental avatar of Nora's lover. Roy's fingers feel like spaghetti when I shake it. I'm ashamed by my satisfaction. He's probably just distracted.

Roy takes me down to the lower deck where the rest of the team is. It is walled in machinery—a tower of monitors and huge monolithic slabs glittered in colored buttons and switches. The machines are tangled in the vines of thick black cables connecting one box to the next. The endless hum of ventilation fans swells in my ears and mutes any other sound. Roy points to a man drawing on a white board in the center of the room. "That's George, the physicist," he yells over the humming. I'm disappointed George isn't wearing a lab coat. He's got gray hair, a thick beard, Clark Kent glasses and wears a flannel shirt. He is drawing two crude airplanes.

His voice is loud and affirmative. "We know the flight paths. If these were two jets colliding at this angle and at this speed, then there's no way what's in that lake is Moncla's jet." The white board flips over to show a map pinned to the other side. An X is marked where the aircrafts had converged on the radar, drawn in thick red marker. Dotted lines show the path of each craft, blue for Moncla and green for the bogey. Our location on the lake is circled in blue as well.

George continues. "Okay, so here's where the math tells us the aircrafts should be." He draws in pencil two possible flight paths. Each crash site is far from our location.

Roy interrupts. "We have to take into account drift at the bottom of the lake over the past fifty years. Not to mention the very high chance that Moncla had control over the plane and was trying to direct it to a safe landing."

This is what Roy wants me here for. He wants to know where Moncla might have been trying to steer the jet, where in 1953 was there a safe place to land. I don't know right away. All eyes are suddenly on me expectantly. I say with as much confidence as I can summon, "I'll need to know the ideal landing conditions for that jet." That seems to appease them. Roy says he'll work with me on this. We're supposed to figure out how a pilot would save his own life after a collision. The only thing I can think of is falling through the sky.

***

Roy and I sit together in a café near the lake during lunch each day of the week. He was a pilot for twelve years. We lay out a new schematic on the table every day. First the whole jet. Then the engines. The wings. The nose. The wheels. Roy explains in detail how much space of flat ground is necessary, how far the plane could glide without power. How far with only the left wing. Or with the right. Or with a certain measurement of wing removed. I take notes on a small map. At the end of each day, we roll out a new map and redraw the potential radius.

I bring the historical documents: records of when Moncla's jet was refueled; the times and dates and distances of his previous two years of flights; transcripts of all air traffic for three months before and after the disappearance. I even dig up all the alien abduction and UFO sighting cases in the area for the surrounding years. I learn that Moncla was married, had a son and a daughter that was born five months before the incident. I wonder if his kids think about their father. I've always wanted kids and Nora always said, "I don't think you're ready." I never knew what that meant, but I nodded along with her and wouldn't bring it up again for a few months. We must have repeated the same discussion thirty times in the last two years.

The Thursday of the second week, Roy puts his coffee down during a break, points at me thoughtfully and says, "You know what's wrong with the official Air Force story?" I make an inquisitive hum in response. "If it was a Canadian bird, there'd be another missing person case, wouldn't there? I mean, that pilot had to have family wondering where the hell he went off to."

"Maybe the Canuck survived the crash?"

"If that bird was good enough to fly back over the border, the radar'd show it leaving our air space. Hell, Moncla's bird should've been spotted too."

"You think it's aliens?"

I've insulted his intelligence. His face is a knot of disgust and offense. "Hell no! I'm not a loon. But it's something. Maybe something we're not cleared to know. Maybe something Canada doesn't want us to know." Roy leans over the table like he's telling me a secret. Ribbons of steam float up from his coffee into his mouth and nostrils. "You know the RCAF were some of the best pilots in World War I? I hear the older guys talking sometimes, their old war stories. The Maple Leaves were called buzzards back then."

"Buzzards?"

"Cause you knew death was storming in the clouds when you saw a Canadian fighter."

Roy doesn't come off as a conspiracy theorist. He's too intelligent. He's told me, for instance, that the F-89 Scorpion piloted by Lt. Moncla had known structural issues in the wing design. An updated model—the F-89D—wouldn't be released until 1954, the year after Moncla's disappearance. The update also fixed a litany of persistent engine problems that plagued previous models. It's an important consideration he says the physicists won't even think about. He claims that even if the pilot was conscious for the entire descent, the engine problems and wing shape would have prevented flying any lengthy distance to safety. We use the historical records to calculate how much fuel Moncla had. We wonder whether the jet's last maintenance check was too long ago, if maybe the jet was doomed to crash even if the bogey didn't exist.

The next day I ask Roy directly where he would have tried to land. The collision point was right near where the two northern tips of Michigan meet at the Canadian border. To the west was Lake Superior and to the east was Lake Erie. South was Lake Michigan. There's a better chance of hitting water than land, but Roy says the plane couldn't go far. "If I'm coming from Kinross, I probably won't be facing a good direction to return."

I agree. Going back west to Kinross increased the likelihood of crashing into rugged terrain. It was wilderness back then, when hills and trees were still a thing.

Roy continues. "Every direction but one also involves water. That's a death trap. There's only one realistic choice."

Most of southern Ontario was cleared of its forestry by the French in the nineteenth century. The land's been flat there for centuries, save for the clusters of strip malls. I ask, "What about the Deceleron?" It was a new type of aileron—those flaps on airplane wings used for landing—that opened up both above and below the wings, clam-style, to act as an air brake.

Roy shrugs. "If he was smart and the wings weren't too badly damaged, they could slow him down. He could've used them to glide for a while."

So we decide together: Canada. It's the only thing that makes sense. Or aliens.

***

The next day, I tell Roy about Nora and he tells me about his divorce. He's been divorced for eight years; he says he's an expert. He says it's a lot like watching a movie at home during a lightning storm. You get invested, absorbed; you forget yourself.

And then the power goes out. The screen is black, the lights are off, the story ends. You still want to know how it ends. He throws a thick finger at me. "That's divorce, Vic. And you just got to learn to get real comfortable in the dark, cause sometimes you don't get to know the story's ending." He laughs like it's a part of the sentence, a punctuation mark to tell me he's trying not to sound bleak.

"Just let it be," he says. "Anything more is just going to hurt you, you know?"

I think Roy is too defeatist. Or maybe he's a womanizer and losing a wife is no big deal; he's got the looks women line up for. I nod along with him anyway. I still try to call Nora when I get home. She doesn't answer. I resent her for giving up the chance to make it work again. I think I can do better this time around. I fantasize of being more assertive, having cheerful conversations with her, buying her flowers. I remember all the fights we've had in the past, the same echoes year after year. She fights; I shut down. Why do I feel like it's my fault? She's the one who had the affair. She's the one who excised all the parts of her life from our life.

***

Nora's been in and out of our home. She still sleeps here every couple of nights. I don't know where she's been staying on the other nights—her lover's or a friend's or a hotel. We don't talk. I know she comes back because she is waiting for me to do something. I chant in my mind to be brave, to make a move and talk to her and try to fix things. My cowardice shames me; I can't even look her in the eyes anymore. I sleep on the couch. In the mornings when she's showering, I can hear her sniffling and sobbing. It echoes in the linoleum sound-box of the bathroom. I wonder if the grief is making her sick. I hear her retching sometimes. On the pillow cases, the silhouettes of her tear stains serve as the phantom traces of our failed romance. I clutch her pillow against my face on the nights she isn't here. It isn't until after I've sucked up all her scent from the fabric that I allow myself to cry.

Nora spent the night last night. It is late afternoon on Saturday. She asks me to take a walk with her. When she passes me on her way to the door, I steal a nostalgic breath of her vanilla scent. We go to a nearby park. It is March and warming into spring, although the dying whispers of winter breeze leave a chill in the air. We walk slowly together side-by-side, so close to one another without touching that anyone could tell we're ex-lovers. My hands are stuffed into my jacket pockets and my eyes trail the ground. She's too beautiful to look at; I keep picturing the plain and pale math nerd from when we met, before she'd learned to straighten her hair or wear make-up or buy clothes that fit properly. I like her better that way. Nora asks, "How is the investigation going?"

I answer, "Nothing's really happening."

"I thought it'd feel like an adventure."

"It really doesn't feel like work. The scientists are still hashing out theories. I provide some records and figures; they try to do the math. Roy thinks his math is better though."

She nods. Silence creeps between us. We sit on a park bench and watch some children on a playground for a few minutes, running and cheering and screaming in glee. Nora's hand moves, floats over mine, then returns to lying flat against her abdomen. I wish she had touched me. It feels like we haven't touched in ages. I ache to return to her intimacy. "Victor," she starts. I cut her off.

"Why are you even here?" I'm surprised by my anger. It's like she's thrown a newspaper on a campfire. I hate the sadness in her voice. She has no right. "Why do you keep coming back?"

"You don't think this is hard for me?"

"No, I don't think this is hard for you. I think you can get whatever you want." Her offense makes it easier to be angry.

She says, "What the hell does that even mean?"

"I mean I fucking think you're being really selfish coming back all the time. I think you get everything. I think you don't give a crap about how much this tortures me." It feels good to argue. I want to hate her. I need to hate her.

The playground children stop to gawk. Parents begin to usher the children away. "God, Victor, I want a life with you. How do you not get this? You know me, Victor. You know me like no one ever has. But you think that being there for me is enough, holding me when I cry or reminding me I'm not that sad girl anymore. And it's not enough, Victor, because you know me and I don't know you, just college Victor. I want you to be my *husband* and it's like you're not even a real person anymore."

"Don't pin this on me. You're the one who was unfaithful."

"God forbid that I wanted to be around someone who actually had a mind of his own." Nora strikes me with a string of words stitched together into a whip. "It's like you can't even decide if you love me or hate me. I love you and it's like you just want a wife. We don't even need to talk or look at each other for you to be happy. It's like having a wife is just a decoration in your life. I can't live like that anymore, *Victor.*" She shapes my name into a dagger at the end of her speech.

I turn away. My head sinks into my shoulders. Her fingertips touch me. She says my name again, kinder this time. I can hear her starting to cry behind me. A sudden thought yanks me back around. Nora stands hands together over her stomach. She doesn't look at me. "You're pregnant, aren't you?" She doesn't answer. I scowl; I can tell she doesn't know who the father is. A bean is in her womb; the life I always wanted is germinating inside her, stewing until it can sprout into a family. I realize suddenly she has the power to steal my whole life and give it to somebody else.

***

On the boat again, we hover above the excavation site. Today the team hauls up the wreckage. If it's Moncla's Scorpion, all of Michigan will know. Everyone moves and talks like they're electrified neurons, saturated in serotonin. They are in the sea, somewhere far away from me. My mind doubles back repeatedly—Nora pregnant. I don't know what to think anymore. Yes, I'll raise the child as my own even if it isn't. If Nora decides to stay. She's left a voicemail this morning. I haven't listened to it. It's like that quantum cat—until the moment I hear her words, I can choose to believe anything and it's equally as true.

When Roy sees me, he slaps my back hard. "Excited to see the scraps?"

It takes me a moment to respond. The sea smells of sewage here. I'm nauseated by the motion. I shrug and try to stare at the horizon. "We both think Moncla landed in Canada. It won't be the Scorpion."

"Anything's possible, Vic."

He leaves my side and approaches the crane that extends from the portside, his cheeks pushed up into golf balls from his grin. He rubs his hands together, bounces on his feet, and I envy his childish enthusiasm. He talks fast into a reporter's microphone, a tangling rope of speech. Incomprehensible. She has to ask him to slow down. It makes him grin wider, baring teeth. She touches his arm—just her fingertips—and jealousy sparks unexpectedly. I don't even know her. Now I see Nora nude, her body pinned by this invisible lover. I cringe.

There's a loud splash. The divers—their wetsuits sheen like their skin is made of oil—emerge slowly from over the ship's edge. The woman peels off her goggles and announces, "Rig's up! Everything's connected."

Roy shouts, "Bring her up!" Gears crank. The giant reel of the crane rolls backward, slurps the steel cables up into a lazy coil. The sound is what you'd expect to hear if machines could fornicate. It gnaws on the ears, but everyone's too excited to care. All eyes are stuck where the cables stab into the water.

Something inside me decides this is the right time to dial my voicemail. The water is spitting forth bubbles; the craft is coming up. I punch in my PIN and press my phone to my ear. My mind throws itself into the sky. I imagine flying the Scorpion, being Moncla, flying closer and closer to the unknown craft. I try to imagine what the bogey might have looked like: a flying saucer, a Canadian jet, another Scorpion. I can't make up my mind; it's just a blob of gray in my head. But there I am, in the air, catapulted at the speed of sound into this goliath mysterious body. All the possibilities open up, images blooming as petals into the black space of my mind. I crash and fly north to Canada. I explode. The bogey teleports me into deep space through a flash of light. My Scorpion spears into Lake Superior and I choke on fire and smoke and water. In that moment, that point of convergence where two flying objects collide, there is nothing but endless sky. There is everywhere to go.

I know I'm not actually the pilot; it's just a fantasy. Nora's the one in the Scorpion and I'm the air traffic controller watching remotely as she flies toward this unknown entity. All I have is a screen that frames the dissolution of my marriage for me.

Metal breaks through the water. The wing is white, glowing from sunlight, streaked with stripes of orange rust. I hear a beep through the phone's speaker. Nora's voice blasts through and collides with my ear like a mallet. I flinch, recoil, almost pull the phone away. But I don't. I hold onto it. I think I want this moment to be the very last of my life—our lives converged in this marriage. A microsecond more, she'll disappear along with that mysterious bogey, that unknown object that flew into my life and cut it in two. All I will see is black.

Conversations with the Rest of the World

The doctors came in droves when Lily was three. White coats who smelled in a way that pricked the inside of her nose with needles and who made her wear heavy uncomfortable blue aprons. They put her inside a tiny room with a one-eyed monster that revolved its head around hers while the ground hummed so deeply she felt her own stomach quake with it.

Later, sitting in her mother's lap, Lily watched one of the doctors move his lips the way her parents did. She read the lip patterns with a hot blade of envy rising in her chest, wondering what magic adults possessed that allowed them to understand each other. When Lily moved her lips in the same way, neither her mother nor father offered the slightest hint of recognition that Lily was understood. On the wall behind the doctor was a framed light that held a piece of black paper and a white glowing picture that looked like a small head with dark swirling shadows in the middle. After watching the doctor point at a whorl of gray on the picture and then Lily's ear, she understood the picture was of Lily herself. The doctor's lips moved in a way she had never seen before, a new pattern and a new idea that she would come to know intimately. His lips stretched into an open line and she could see the tip of his tongue pressed to the roof of his mouth. When his tongue released, his upper teeth met his lower lip. The new word he spoke was one that would hinge onto Lily for her whole life; it was her identity: deaf.

***

At the age of four, Lily was introduced to a young pretty woman named Miss Rachel, the first person Lily had ever met besides her parents and those doctors who poked inside her ear all the time. Miss Rachel had thick-framed rectangular glasses, blonde hair that was always tied back, and wore an assortment of colorful dresses with skirts that moved like thin curtains swaying in the wind.

On the first day, Miss Rachel handed Lily an apple and then took it away. She immediately started crying and Miss Rachel made a closed hand, pressing her index knuckle against her cheek, and pivoted her hand back and forth. At the same time, she mouthed the word Lily knew was apple—first an open and round mouth, next the lips met and a puff of air burst through to open the lips once more. Lily continued to weep and Miss Rachel showed her the apple once more. With her free hand, she performed the odd gesture again. And again. And again. Until Lily's tears had long stopped and she began to watch the ritual with curiosity, and then finally mimicked the movement herself. Miss Rachel clapped and smiled brightly and nodded with fervor as she handed Lily the apple. This time, she did not take it away. It took all week for Lily to understand that this gesture also meant apple and that her hands had the power to telegraph her thoughts.

***

Her father put records on from time to time and moved in the living room in a jerky way that Lily never understood until one day when she positioned herself on the ground very near to the speakers and felt upon her flesh a magical confluence of vibrations—the bass, in short staccatos, reverberating through the hollow of her spine and the harmonics of the treble licking at her skin like static shocks. She placed her tiny palms right against the speaker's fabric net and felt the hums converge together, a dozen lines of sound melting into soup. She pressed her back up to the speakers sometimes, let the music under the chamber of her chest and watched as her father danced himself to the beat, swaying his hips and tapping his feet. He was a tall and thin man, short cropped brown hair, and limbs that were long and angular so that when he danced, there was always a sacred geometry mapped by his body.

***

Miss Rachel was not only her signing tutor, but was to be her kindergarten teacher as well. In her first month of school, Lily and her class went to the zoo. At each pen Lily tried her hardest to lean over the railing in order to get as close as possible to each majestic creature. The class passed birds of every color and size. Their tour guide, dressed in a sand-colored safari get-up and a pith helmet, signed brief descriptions of the animals at each pen. There was a whole path walled by pens of bizarre hooved creatures to either side: camels whose hairy backs looked like mounds of hay and antelope crowned with spiraling horns and some strange beast Lily had never seen before that looked like a cross of ox, deer and goat. The class walked along a high bridge suspended over a vast field of green where in the distance giraffes' heads nested peacefully on the canopies of their tree trunk necks. All the hooved animals smelled like the stuff the dog left behind in the lawn and the children began to sign to one another, You smell like a camel! They did this with each new animal and burst into fits of giggles. And, after an hour of walking and stopping and gawking, the class arrived at the primate pen where a family of gorillas was grooming each other quietly.

Lily leaned over the railing. The gorilla pen was rather large and contained in a black wire fence. Between the fence and the overlook railing, her body was now slung over a moat of running water that created a barrier between the two. She squinted in disbelief across the distance, trying to affirm what she thought she saw. Some of the gorillas were making signs with their hands. Now the other children leaned forward. They recognized it too. A dozen tiny heads turned to face their tour guide. As he spoke, he signed. His hands told of the puzzle pieces of life called DNA and how the difference between human and ape was like taking a tiny fraction off only one puzzle piece. Lily marveled.

The zookeeper continued. He signed: A long time ago, scientists taught a couple of gorillas sign language. Remarkably, they learned it. It isn't perfect, but you can make it out. If you have little brothers or sisters, it is a lot like signing to a three year old. They even teach it to their babies now. We try harder every year to increase their understanding. Just imagine what it would be like if humans could actually have conversations with the rest of the world. What would the animals tell us, do you think? That's what the scientists do here: teach enough so that one day the gorillas might tell us how we're doing with this whole ruling the world business.

Draping her body over the railing, her mouth hung open. When she looked back for her mother—who was chaperoning the trip—she could see her engaged in conversation with Miss Rachel.

Miss Rachel said, I always love coming here. It's breathtaking. I can't imagine what it's like for the children, to see another species communicating in their native language.

Lily looked back to the apes. Yes, they were signing to each other! The big beast—the mother—was signing to her children, Come. Groom.

Lily leapt excitedly, wildly waving her hands. Hello! Hello!

One young gorilla, no bigger than she was, crawled up to the edge of the gorilla pen and gazed up at her from where the moat began. The gorilla responded, Hello human. Then it bared its teeth and fangs which shocked Lily before she calmed and realized it was smiling at her.

She signed, How are you?

Lily grinned so hard her face hurt. The young gorilla looked like a large infant. Its head was mostly bald; the black hair on its crown was a thin wiry patch of translucent tangles like the dust clouds Lily found underneath the couch. Its eyes were big, round, and surprisingly human-like. She had expected the glassy eyes of her dog, the dumb expression that revealed nothing but the simplest desires: food, play, joy. Even her mother had given the same vacant look before, as if someone had gone and scrubbed out the inside of her head. This most often happened at the doctor's when the white coats were speaking to her mother for a long time in lip patterns Lily couldn't recognize. Sometimes, she'd giggle and try to wake her mother up by tugging at a sleeve or a wisp of her hair or her necklace. Then through some sudden sorcery, her mother's eyes would reignite.

The gorilla signed back, *Happy. Sign human big. No small.*

Lily thought for a second, piecing together the fragmented ideas in her head. She was used to having to reorganize ideas. Before Miss Rachel taught her to sign, she often tried to communicate by combining and recombining lip patterns in different orders to see if her parents could understand better or even recognize her attempts at communication. She did the same here, rearranging the words until she decided that the gorilla was telling her it was happy to be signing with a child. Lily turned around, glee engraving a grin on her lips as she waved excitedly to her classmates. They rushed the railing and a chorus of small hands gestured frantically to the beasts.

The jaws of each gorilla split into smiles and open laughter. They raised their hands.

***

Every weekend her father took her to the park. In the distance, two basketball courts took up half the park which Lily and her father always avoided. The young boys all gathered there in contest like gladiators. The other half of the park—their half—was an open field of grass, all green save for patches of sandy dirt freckling the ground. There was a playground in the corner of the field that called to Lily. She raced toward it every weekend, leaving her father on a bench. Her eyes absorbed its architecture. There were swing sets and seesaws and her favorite piece of equipment was a bright red jungle gym sprouting from the earth in a twisted knot of metal. Lily bounced on ground that looked like hard asphalt yet yielded beneath her feet in a strange rubbery way.

Sometimes her father took her into the grass and they threw a baseball between themselves. Most weekends, he sat on the bench and read business magazines when Lily made her dash toward the playground. She always climbed the jungle gym. Climbed and climbed. And when at last she reached the summit of the red tower, she sat across two bars, tiny legs dangling, and watched over the entire park. The bodies below were small and Lily felt a tremendous calm looking down over the park.

At first, Lily tried to play with other children in the park. They were welcoming enough, inviting her in when she noticed their lips moving at her. Eventually though, they stopped. She could see from her high tower perch their lips whispering comments about the weird girl who never spoke. They whispered and then they watched her and then they whispered some more. When they noticed her eyes from above, they turned their backs. Sometimes Lily avoided looking at their mouths. Sometimes she couldn't help herself.

***

It was amusing to watch when Lily's father finally relented to lessons in sign, to see his eyes glow hot with frustration when he failed. As far as it mattered to her, sound was still magic, still a supernatural sense. She saw how dependent her father was on sound, how he needed it to organize his world. Their first conversations were simple. At dinner, he asked how Lily's food was. She moved to reply, but her father's nose had already descended to his plate. The line of Lily's lips fell into a frown. She knew it meant nothing; she had already come to understand that the mysticism of sound was that it was not sight. People could transmit thoughts without their gaze. She saw in school the hearing children taking turns over food. One spoke and the other ate. When Lily signed to Miss Rachel, Miss Rachel became her whole world.

Her mother smiled warmly and pulled back the brunette hair that fell over her face. Lily smiled back. Her mother signed, How was your school day?

Good, replied Lily. The new teacher is having trouble teaching us to read though. I'm glad Miss Rachel still comes here.

Lily was learning to read. Miss Rachel told her that once she learned how to write a sentence, almost anyone would be able to understand her. And so she began trying to glue the written words to her brain, studying the careful shapes of letters and how they interacted with one another to create ideas. But this was a struggle—as soon as she felt she had a grasp on a word, casting the text's font into the folds of her mind, she would look away from the page and all the letters would dissolve into hills of black sand.

Her mother signed back, It must be hard. Words are in different orders than what you're used to.

And Lily responded with mild offense: They come in the same way that people speak. I read lips all the time. I'm used to that, but not these shapes.

Her mother just didn't get it. Miss Rachel had informed Lily that hearing children sounded words out when they learned to read. How could Lily hope to even understand what this meant? Reading and writing were conventions made for the hearing. Written language was predicated on sound and she was learning English as a set of pictograms, memorizing whole shapes to represent words and never learning how those words were built. She understood the lip patterns of letters and shapes, but little more.

When Lily and her mother had conversations in the past, her father often sat silently. She could always see the perturbed glint in his eyes, the hidden snarl behind the flat line of his lips, the whole electric aura that radiated from his skin to hers in nasty bitter heat. Longing for her father blistered in her belly. They were always so far apart, mute to each other. But she noticed, too, how her father didn't speak much to her mother either, how they often passed each other by with sheepish smiles in the kitchen or in the hall, how her mother read in the bedroom upstairs and he watched the television downstairs.

After her father forked a bite into his mouth, Lily signed again when he looked up. Immediately he stiffened and an embarrassed pink flushed his cheeks as he realized his folly. He set his fork down in a jerky hesitant movement. In reply, he signed, Sorry. Lily smiled.

Her mother's lips moved to say, Thank you for trying, Bruce.

Her father replied, I feel like an idiot.

Learning a whole new language is tough, said Lily's mother. It'll come. It was hard for me too. It still is.

Lily turned back to her food and ate. She let her parents recede from her world; she let them saunter casually back to their own without the intrusion of her gaze.

***

Her father took her to the zoo one day after weeks of begging and pleading. She took his hand and sprinted toward the gorilla pen, jerking him along behind her. The young gorilla she had first signed with—named Hermes by the zookeepers—was engaged in a conversation with an older female gorilla. She signed, No game.

Hermes replied, Give food. The female repeated herself emphatically. It looked like Hermes was explaining himself: Game gorillas, food give.

Lily looked up at her father. He squinted and leaned himself forward. She smiled, hope bursting inside of her. Maybe he could decipher the message too. But he turned his gaze back down to her and signed, It's just gibberish.

She shook her head. No, they just don't know the right order. Lily began waving toward Hermes until she had his attention. She signed, Do you remember me? This is my father.

Hermes smiled and replied, Hello human-small. Hello human-big.

She nudged her father. She signed, Have a conversation. Ask him how he is.

Her father was stoic. He stared at Hermes who started signing something about crushed apples. Then he looked back down at Lily and signed, They can't actually communicate. They're just animals, Lily. They're trained with a few words and that's it.

She frowned. The gorillas could communicate. She looked over the pen and saw four separate conversations. But there was the railing, the chasm that had been dug out to create a moat of water and an impassable barrier between the humans and the gorillas. An image descended into Lily's mind of herself floating in the moat, the great gulf built on a fraction of a puzzle piece. When she looked up at her father, she imagined a railing under his nose.

***

When Lily rushed down the stairs in the morning, turned the corner to cross through the living room into the kitchen, she saw her father on the couch, his body made a fat sausage beneath a blue blanket. She touched his face and he awoke with a start. He smiled, but his eyes were puffy like he had cried all night. A yellow crust bridged over his eye, connected together his lashes until Lily plucked it away. Her father sat up, folded his arms around her, the blanket cocooning the pair together. Then he stood and Lily watched as his body rounded back the corner to the stairs from which she came.

At the breakfast table, Lily's mother did not sign a greeting to her. There was just a pleasant smile, although it appeared drawn on her face because her eyes were not reacting to her lips. Lily normally felt her mother was beautiful, admired the rich chocolate imbued into her eyes and hair. Today there was purple rubbed in beneath her eyes. She looked haggard. Her gaze never touched Lily again that morning—always, they were either on plates or silverware or food or the clock. When her father returned, dressed and groomed, Lily saw that neither set of lips moved. She saw the quick darting glances her parents stole of each other, the momentary diagonal line their mouths formed, how the muscles that controlled their faces were held slack such that even their eyes seemed to sag. Their bodies radiated a heat of quiet animosity which found form as a sore in Lily's stomach.

A new fact about sound was learned at this breakfast table: silence was a punishment. And then there was last night, when the vibrations had channeled through the floorboards. There were quick strong, rapid booms—a series of stomps like her father marching across the room, his disquiet dragging itself along the wooden planks and then inching up Lily's ankles. She placed her hand upon the wall and felt mild buzzing akin to when she would hold a tin can to Miss Rachel's mouth and have her sing into it. Lily went to her door, cracked it open, peeked through the hallway to see her parents' bedroom open, the light on, her mother's face flushed pink, wet with tears, and she was shouting. Her lips read, If you don't love me anymore, why are you even here?

Now her father stepped into Lily's view. He stared down her mother, more menacing a glare than Lily had ever seen him wear. He spoke slowly, Why do you think? Then he turned toward the hallway. Her father threw the door shut as he left the room. The sound pulsed through the air with violence. The boom bloated in Lily's belly, and then sat there to stagnate.

***

Her father signed, The dog bit me today.

Grinning, Lily asked, Really?

No, I just learned bite, he responded. She giggled, felt the hum of it in her throat, saw her father smiling to the sight—or maybe the sound. All the same, it warmed her when he smiled. There had been little smiling lately from her father or her mother. Just yesterday, Lily went to hug her father's waist in the morning before school. He knelt and met her eyes and his weeping came on suddenly, his eyes and his lips all pulled down and when he hugged Lily to his body, she felt his breathing as a series of jolting pops. More and more, it was like this. Any interaction—like their weekend park trip—seemed forced and his affection feigned. He was always somewhere else. He sat on the bench with his spine sloped like a question mark, his eyes slowly drifting away from whatever was happening, always toward some pocket of attention inside his head.

This is my *deaf* daughter, he told a woman last weekend. The woman blinked in shock, stiffened unnaturally, and then gave a sweeping and overdone show of sympathy. Lily hated the woman for it. When she looked back to her father, she saw how he had stitched a smile over his face. His words were superficially cheerful; his lips revealed a private calamity.

***

And then he was gone. His drawers emptied. His toothbrush vanished. He left behind a scribble on a scrap of paper left on the kitchen table. For all of Lily's progress in reading, she could only make sense of trivial words. *I'm. Go. My. You. The.* Miss Rachel, when she heard the news, showered Lily with sympathetic attention. Her mother lavished her with toys and treats—Oreos and peanut butter cups and ice cream sandwiches.

It didn't stop the confusion.

Lily tried figure out this new order, but the pieces didn't fit. They jarred inside her. She clung to memories of her father, retreating to the empty basement at night, sliding chairs across the floor so she could climb atop them and finger the padded hooks of the now barren wall mounts. Shadow outlines of guitars stained the walls. Each day, she returned home to find more and more relics of her phantom father receding from their home. The albums all vanished in a day, leaving square slots naked. It was unsettling to be able to see the wall so easily through the shelf. Her mother later placed banal ornaments in their place: snow globes, small picture frames, a tiny porcelain statue of a gorilla they had purchased on the zoo trip. It felt to Lily like blowing air into the spaces left by her father.

Miss Rachel continued to visit at least two evenings a week.

Lily felt it was as much for herself as her mother. When Lily asked of her father, Miss Rachel only replied that he went away. Her mother wouldn't reply at all.

***

One day at school, in the cafeteria where the children ate lunch, Lily had spotted a table of children all propped up with their knees on their seats, leaning their bodies hungrily over the table and passing a pair of dice between them. One child shook his fist into the air and dropped the dice. All the children then roared up, cocking their heads back with jaws agape in laughter. Lily approached and peered between the heads and shoulders of children. On the table was a board with an arrangement of colored squares. A number of the squares had tiny colored plastic pieces resting atop them and, at the board's center, two thick decks of cards stood side-by-side like skyscrapers over the pieces.

Lily gently nestled her way between bodies, eager to join in their game. The boy across the table met her gaze. He asked, Who's the girl?

A brunette girl beside him answered, I think she's one of the deaf kids from the Special Hall. I've seen her around.

Lily thought that the kids kept chattering on about her, but she couldn't move her eyes fast enough to catch anyone's lips. She followed their eyes though, moving from one child to another. There was definitely a conversation. Finally, she saw the first boy say: Ignore her. She can watch all she wants. We don't have to let her play.

With that, another child launched the dice onto the board. Lily turned away, withdrawing back to her table with her classmates where she felt some semblance of *normal*. She should have been used to it, the way the children in the park had come to exclude her. Today, she felt weak. Today, the weight of her isolation was crushing. Today, the world felt especially cruel, especially unfair, especially volatile.

Distraught, bewildered, Lily rushed home at the day's end, sped up the stairs and into her room, waiting until the sun set and cast her room, the hall, the house in darker shades of blue. Waiting until she saw light bleed up the stairwell to tell her that her mother had finally returned home. And then Lily descended in a fury, tears streaming and hands frantic. A blur of fingers and knuckles and fists. Her mother hugged her and Lily drank in the scent of strawberry-melon shampoo, nestled her face into her mother's shoulder and hair.

Later, after she had calmed, Lily signed, It will always be this way, won't it? I'm a freak. And then she collapsed into a puddle on the carpet.

Her mother stroked Lily's hair and mouthed in front of her eyes, You are incredibly special. Now she pulled away, held Lily by the shoulders and her face grew grave so that Lily knew to pay attention. She spoke with her lips this time: I want you to understand, Lily, that none of this is your fault.

But Lily was not so sure. For all of her ability to pick up a conversation from across the room, to read the buried twists and twitches of a person's lips, there were things she could never hear or understand: how she cleaved the love between her mother and father in two; what dug the vast lacuna between her father and herself; how being human felt.

***

Weeks later, Miss Rachel took Lily back to the zoo. She wanted to see the gorillas again. Lily stood at the railing and gazed down over the beasts, watching their conversations. The gorillas signed in shards of words and ideas and metaphors that made her laugh breathlessly to herself. The younger apes signed upward to the humans on the overlook, trying desperately to be understood. Lily signed down, Hello, friends!

Frantically, the gorillas signed their responses, simple words and ideas that described their moods and desires.

Lily watched the fragmented conversations of the animals. She imagined a future life: Lily, the adult; Lily, the scientist; Lily, the bridge between humanity and the rest of the world. Maybe someday, between her mother and father too. She imagined ripping away all the invisible railings in the world, all the barriers to speaking up. She saw herself filling up that moat with dirt, mud, soil, and all the richness of the earth.

The Dharma's Hand

We hiked six kilometers to reach the ruptured earth that would lead us into Son Doong. At nine kilometers long, it was the largest cave in the world—large enough to support an entire jungle ecosystem. The cave had only been open to tourists for a couple of years now; everything below was still wild. The mouth was a rim of rock the color of clay. The ledges all leaned into each other, not like a fissure split open or collapsed inward, but like wounded flesh closing up. It was a disorienting feeling, staring into that earthly scar; there was an entire sky between the rock you stood on and the forest that flowered below.

My brother Phong was kneeling behind us, hammering steel stakes into the stone floor. "Nuts, right? Wonder how it formed."

"Nuts," I agreed.

Our father was to be our tour guide through the cave. This was the last leg of our trip, the part of it meant for me and my healing. We'd spent the last two weeks with family. We'd met Ba's other child for the first time, a woman ten years older than us named Thi with a little girl of her own. When I had Thi's daughter bouncing on my knee, the girl's round face in open-mouthed glee, I'd felt a pang of sorrow. I handed her back only after a moment.

Right now Ba was standing with his leg propped up on a rock, facing the forest below with his back to us. Despite Ba being a short elderly man, he looked like an adventurer right then, his fists stapled to his hips by the knuckles. He looked large, like he'd conquered the cave, the mountain, the country itself a dozen times before. I could almost picture a saber hanging from his hip. Ba answered, "They said water from river make limestone go away. Until it collapse into cave. Instant sunroof."

Ba was always a mythic sort of man. As children, when we came down with colds, Ba sat us down on the ground in front of him and had us remove our shirts. He'd use a quarter dipped in a green potion and scraped the metal edge in lines across our backs. This was the *cao gió* ritual. These lines would seethe and burn and we'd carry the cool mint vapor with us everywhere we went, each breath bringing calm relief. I remembered Phong's back was always left with a ladder of bright red rows gashed across his skin. Ba said that sickness came from dark magic, that the coin could release the black energies ensnared by the body. Within an hour, our stuffed noses could breathe freely. Our heads cleared. The soreness in our throats softened.

This was the magic of our father, the lost sorcery of our culture. He'd been trained as a *thầy pháp*, a conjurer, a mystic hand of dharma. I always considered myself secular and critical, not prone to the same superstitions as most other Vietnamese, but I could never not be awed by Ba. Even now in his seventies, he had more strength and vitality than me. I have never doubted it was due to his training in the mystic arts.

I felt a tug on my harness as Phong hooked me up. I looked over my shoulder, he gave me a thumbs up, and then I looked into the hole. I could see birds flying around above the tree tops, blues ones and red ones and if I squinted I could just pick out the green ones. I turned back around and started leaning onto my heels until the line went taut. Then I let myself drop.

The rappel was a smooth fast ride until I reached the bottom of the fissure where the vertical wall of rock suddenly receded into a massive dome of dirt. I looked up and Phong bellowed down, "The line's good. You just need to abseil the rest. Slowly." The drop was about forty meters by my guess. Despite being a gentle glide down, I was grateful the moment my feet touched ground.

In front of me was the forest. The trees were as tall as any on the surface, but the trunks bent and weaved erratically, leaning and snaking to catch any of the light that might spill over from the remnants of rock ceiling. As my brother and father descended, I took the time to look behind me and saw the faint blue glow of whatever luminescent microbes were painting the wet walls in the distance, dust constellated onto darkness.

When everyone was down, Ba rubbed his hands clean of debris and then grabbed the set of cords we rode down on. He pulled from the bundle a white rope with blue threading. He said in Vietnamese, "We use to this to get back up when we're done." And then he began walking into the woods without another word. Though it was daylight, a great shadow of the stone ceiling stretched across the jungle and I couldn't be sure of where the light was, when we would next see a band of sun beaming into this underworld.

Olivia had been pregnant, but she never wanted kids. The night she told me, I noticed her missing as I readied for bed. I found her outside of our apartment complex. She was standing beside the building in her bathrobe dragging a cigarette. There was a storm rolling through the clouds, a cerulean vortex sucking up sunlight from the sky and draining daylight into dusk. I stood beside her silently. We watched the sky together. I waited for a clap of thunder, a crack of lightning, the crash of water colliding into concrete. The clouds kept whirling and I thought of towels spinning in a washer. Before we married, I promised her I was okay with never having children. I just assumed she'd change her mind later; I was always told women turned around on the baby thing as they aged. But she was never going to change her mind. The embryo was an infection she feared would slowly rot away her life.

After an hour, I touched her forearm. I drenched my voice with affective concern and asked, "Are you okay, honey? What're you doing out here?"

She answered, "I'm waiting for the rain."

I asked, "Why?"

She said, "I'm thinking about something."

Her face was suddenly long when she looked at me. Streetlight painted us orange. The thick down of fog layered liquids on our skin and I couldn't tell if the beads of water pimpling her face were sweat or tears. She tangled her fingers with mine and led me back to our door. She said, "Come on, dear. Let's go inside," as if I was the one who needed comforting.

***

The soil squished beneath our feet at times; other times we stood on slabs of stone carpeted in moss. There were no paths, only clusters of trees or small clearings or ponds gulping a rush of falling water like white foam hailing from the heavens. Our heaven, in this case, was a canopy of rock. Phong on occasion dropped us a factoid he'd read on the flight here. He mentioned once that Son Doong Cave belied another cave above for much of its length. This cave carried a run of water diverged from the river. So there was a river on the surface that became a river buried that became a twice-buried pond situated in a jungle below the earth.

Phong asked, "What creatures do we find down here?"

"*Nhiều loài động vật*," said Ba. Many animals.

"Any predators?" I asked.

He shrugged and nodded. "*Có, nó có.*"

Phong and I both stopped and stared at him. We waited. He laughed and remained silent. He walked onward. Phong asked, "Okay, what predators?"

Ba laughed again. "*Hai đứa con sợ, ha?*" He punctuated his words with heavy breaths. The air was thicker down here, the humidity so great that each suckle of air was a chore.

I replied, "We are not afraid. It'd just be nice to know what can eat us down here."

He turned his head, looked over his shoulder at us. "*Cá sấu,*" he said. I looked at my brother; he looked at me. Phong shrugged and then I shrugged and we looked back at our father. Ba groaned and then grunted in English, "Crocodile." He stretched his hands away from each other, just about a meter, and said, "But very small." Ba pointed at a shrub, blossoming with yellow flowers spreading spear-shaped petals. "*Hoa là* more dangerous."

Phong and I traded a worried look, but said nothing else. No one spoke again for some time. We followed behind Ba, mesmerized by his superhuman endurance. We were the sport cavers, not him, but he walked through the jungle like it was his home. And for the first time in a long time—since I moved in with Olivia years ago—I felt safe. Here in the world my parents came from. Here, lost within the world's longest cave, shielded from the life I left by cliffs of stone and my father's sorcery.

As we hiked, the song of our sighing, our grunts and occasional spitting accompanied the jungle's music. Every so often, one of us would cough or sneeze. We scrambled up lean-tos of slate-gray boulders from which sprouted trees of gnarled white-gray bark. Some trunks appeared as a twisted weave of several trees, but when we climbed upon the rocks they grew on, it was easy to see how the bark did not sever, only bent at angles. As we went on, the trees became fewer and fewer. Rock formations towered around us in their place, dressed with skins of algae anywhere the sun could reach. And further down, the great stones hovering over us became shallower, the floor rose and recessed, a scattering of mole hills and saddles leading deeper into the dark earth. The field of algae beneath our feet ceased as we descended. From here on, green came in patches, splattered across a sea of blues and blacks and browns.

Ba turned the flashlight on his belt on. Phong and I did the same. We decided to rest for a moment. We freed from our packs a handful of protein bars that we unwrapped and ate. Phong asked Ba, "I never understood. Why did you leave your first wife and Thi to come to the US?"

His expression went long for a moment. He answered, shaking his head slowly, "Không có choice." He smiled sadly. He told us about the siege of his city, the news coming in through telephone wire declaring the loss of the nation, the realization that he could either stay and fight and die or board the boat ferrying refugees to the American allies.

Something twisted up in my stomach. I bit my lower lip. I scratched at my arm. A rash was forming on my skin, speckles of red coming to the surface. Poison ivy, I figured. We both turned from the crater's center, walked in circles around it gathering driftwood logs that must've washed in from rainfall back where the sky was opened. We lay them down at the center to use as benches.

As Ba lowered himself slowly to a sit, he let out another laugh. He said, "Old man now."

Phong and I traded another look. I knew we were asking the same questions. How could our father grow old? How could he weaken? He was superhuman. Magical. A demigod. I wondered, if his body could weaken, did that mean his magic could too?

***

I received a text from Olivia one day while I was at work.

I didn't want to look at it. I had felt the seed inside her splitting us apart for weeks now. I came home from work with a half-dozen yellow roses the other day. She smiled and kissed my cheek and hung the roses upside-down on the wall to wilt and wither. When we went to bed, I tried to spoon with her. She twisted and turned beneath the weight of my limply draped arm. She squeezed herself free from me. She said she was getting too warm. I rolled away and we slept with our backs facing one another.

I didn't look at her text for hours, as if whatever words were there could not exist without my consent. And yet they did exist, digital data stagnating in my pocket. Somewhere between Olivia and myself—beamed into space by satellite, saturating all air along that phantom path—were her words. And yet I still ignored, despite how her ghostly words stuck to my skin.

I didn't look until I had to come home.

And then I looked. She said we needed to talk. When I walked through the doorway, she was sitting at the dinner table. The lights were dimmed to gentle orange. The walls looked stained with rust. Shadows stretched from her brows over her eyes. From the shadows bled mascara that blackened her cheeks. We talked.

She had lost the seedling. She wasn't sorry. She didn't want another. She didn't want the life I wanted for us.

It was done. So were we.

***

Inside the sleeve of stone, there was no sky above us. Darkness stretched so far and high that we could not see the rock roofing over our heads. Son Doong was rich with cave pearls—orbs of minerals calcified on crags and in crevices—that salted the distant ceiling. They captured the lights bleeding from the bulbs at our belts and returned them to us as luminescent glitter, a simulacrum of the night sky complete with its own cartography of constellations. And though there was no sun, life resolved; here the algae returned, slicking the ground green such that it felt as if we were in a palace of jade. As our soles crushed that carpet beneath us, a musk much like mold sprayed up to our noses. Our tunnel, as wide as a four-lane highway, then opened up to a goliath chamber whose perimeters stretched further than our eyes could reach. We were greeted with a crude imitation of the surface: a vast emerald field, the illusion of stars scattered across an endless open sky, a violent hush of water from a river somewhere in the distance and, overtop, the melody of alien life buzzing, chirping, croaking, squealing. We could see no end. My jaw hung slack. Some small carapaced creature flew into it. I gagged and spat. Ba laughed at me, and then Phong joined him.

Ba mockingly dusted his hands. "Set camp here," he said. "Cannot see, but sun is setting." He unclipped his backpack and set it at his feet. He began to unstrap the nylon tube his tent was stuffed inside.

We had collected timber as we walked through the forest. Phong gathered it and made a bundle of it and lit it ablaze with a lighter. We unwrapped protein bars and chewed for ages.

I asked Ba, "Does it bother you? Not having grandkids yet?"

He held his open palms to the fire. I half-expected it to flare up, like he was casting another spell. He gave me a confused look. I turned my eyes away, down to the flames. Ba said, "No, boy. Having *cháu* not important. Just happiness."

I nodded but didn't respond. I thought briefly of Thi and her young daughter, of staying here in this strange land, of being an uncle rather than a father. Phong knew, of course. A brother always knows your thoughts. He said, "Don't even think about it. Ma would kill you."

I laughed. "Yeah. Yeah, she would."

Phong and I had wanted to visit Viet Nam since we were kids. As soon as we were both out of college, we started making plans and saving money. We told Ma about it one day, thinking she'd be delightfully surprised; she wasn't. We were having dinner together in Ma's house. She sat across the table from me. The smile I wore when I told her was so wide I can remember the muscle ache in my cheeks.

Her eyes widened. She turned her face away from mine and toward the ground at her side. "You are not ready to *đi về nhà* Viet Nam, con."

Phong started laughing. "What? Why not? I can speak enough Vietnamese to get by."

"No, con." She shook her head. "*Không có* about language."

"Then what is it?" I asked.

She paused. Her lips were slashed across her face in a diagonal. She replied, "I do not know how to say to you in English. You will not understand. *Người* Viet Nam, they can do something to you. We call it '*bỏ bùa*.'"

Phong turned his head away, held his hands to his mouth, stifling an obvious fit of giggles. When he composed himself, he asked, "You're afraid someone will bewitch us?"

Ma straightened in her seat. She pointed a finger at Phong. "Yes," she said excitedly. "That is the word. Bewitch." She said it with a space between the syllables—*bee witch*. "They go after men like you, *người* Viet Nam from America who do not believe in the old magic."

I'd heard stories of the sorceresses who could enslave the minds of men. Their magic came from a minority ethnic group, either from the Khmer or the Thai, and involved binding a spirit to a mystical flower. The flower's pollen could then be collected, rendered a fine powder that enchanted any person unlucky enough to touch it. I always thought the stories were a way for a man to pardon his lust, claiming a witch had taken him for a weekend, when in fact he was at a whorehouse fucking some charlatan.

Ma's face at that moment, though—I'd only seen that face once before, when Ba woke up one day, half his face slackened, half his body unmoving. We rushed him to the hospital. He'd come down with a stroke-like condition called Bell's palsy. Only temporary, the doctor said. But Ma in that room, looking down at Ba in that bed, she wore the same face. It was fear marred across her skin. It was abject terror.

She made us swear on her life we'd never go to Viet Nam without Ba to protect us against dark magic. And so when it came time, we made sure to keep our word.

Ba crawled into his tent before we did ours. Phong asked me through a whisper, "How are you feeling?" I shrugged. "This is the cave drop of a life time, man."

"We had a whole life," I said. I didn't let my eyes move from the now-dying flames.

"And now you have your life back," said Phong. "And it's all yours."

***

When I first moved in with Olivia—before the child and before the marriage—the ornaments of my home had been re-appropriated into hers. She had bought a house early on, before the market crash and straight out of college with her parents' assistance. It was a longer commute to work, but it felt natural that a husband and wife should own a house. This was the narrative of an American life; a single adult was a sad alien creature, worse if not a homeowner, worse still if not a parent. I put most of my effects in the basement, lined the walls with my collection of guitars, and tried to resituate. But I missed my old apartment, my five years in it, the occasional rain of stucco dust when the young woman who lived above me brought home a man for a one-night stand. I missed the smell of the kitchen, even if that scent often was old soapy dishwater. It had been mine. And suddenly I was sleeping in a foreign bed in a foreign room, putting my laundry away into the drawers of Olivia's dresser that she'd cleared out for me; I was expected to call this new world home. I had nothing in that house except a wife and a basement.

***

My stomach growled itself into a hard knot that pried me from sleep and wet my eyes and forced a frown onto my face. We disassembled our camp. We were taking a different path back to the forest by following the river. All the fun parts of caving were to begin because we were running out of food, the way Phong and I always planned when we caved. The last stretch of hiking and the occasional rock scramble would be the most arduous in our exhaustion. We walked mostly in silence, passing a canteen among ourselves to sip from and sucking from tubes of carbohydrate gels throughout the day. I did my best not to think about home, to focus on this dark world around me.

Over the course of several hours, I noticed the rhomboid heads of white fish schooling inside the luminescent oval of my flashlight when I dragged it over the water's surface. They were small fish, no bigger than the palm of a hand, so unnaturally white their scales looked coated in chalk. The fish weren't albinos; they just had no reason to keep producing pigments in the darkness.

Cavern wildlife tended to be white; Son Doong Cave was no different. All the creatures we encountered were seemingly skinned with snow: the moths and the dragonflies, the lizards and geckos, the frogs and toads. Color had no place in this world.

Dusk came slowly. Due to the darkness, I didn't notice when the distant rocky ceiling was no longer above us. My eyes were always ahead or down and the tunnel's mouth must have been wider than I could see because there had been no clear distinction between cave and jungle. At some point the algae became clovers and small weeds, though in the darkness I couldn't spot a difference. The sound of the river stream saturated my ears for so long I didn't notice when the buzzing of insects accompanied it. And so I didn't notice either when the quiet intermittent chirps of distant birds too became audible. When we stopped to set camp again, I looked upward and saw the familiar screen of velvet with its glowing white dust, and resigned to another night sandwiched between layers of stone. I dropped my backpack and set out the items we'd need in the morning. We shared two protein bars between the three of us and set up small tents of plastic sheets to collect dew overnight to replenish our water.

Ba asked, "*Hai đứa con làm này* for fun? Crazy boys." He punctuated his comment with another roll of his grunting laughter. Neither Phong nor I answered. We knew to conserve energy. We both were panting. Ba's dark brown skin was slicked in a layer of sweat, but his breaths were still long and slow and he kept on laughing at us. He said, "Of course you tired. All you think about is the end. Getting back home. But what is difference between now and when we start?" He was grinning as he spoke, like he was showing off that he could breathe where we struggled. "No difference. When you walk, know you are walking. Cannot think of the end. That make you focus on pain. Cannot think of how long you walk. That make you focus on pain too. Walking one hour or six hours, no difference. One step is always one step."

It reminded me of when we took him to eat these hot wings that required you sign a waiver. The waiter brought out three small black plates, a single wing in glowing orange sauce a piece. Phong and I took a bite each. It felt like napalm spreading out over the surface of your tongue. I guzzled my water glass. I tried to wipe as much of it off my tongue as I could with a napkin. Each second that passed, the heat intensified. My brother and I were both in tears, watching our father slowly finish his wing off, then Phong's, and then mine. He carefully wiped the sauce from his hands and mouth with a wet nap. Next came his familiar guttural laugh. He said in Vietnamese, "These crazy Americans. Why make something so spicy?" Later, when we could speak again, we asked him how he managed to finish all three wings. He said the same sort of thing: "If you take one bite, why not two? There is no difference."

I unrolled my sleeping bag, which now smelled of sulfur and mold, and ignored how wet it was, because everything was wet and hot here, and lay atop it. I did my best to ignore the acid ache in my thighs, the piercing hunger, the thirst-made roughness in my throat. I had expected my misery to suspend sleep for an hour or more, but after just a moment, exhaustion conquered all maladies and I slept like solid stone.

I woke up to sunlight and only then did I realize that I had seen stars, not cave pearls, before sleep. I got up and looked ahead of us on the path, seeing lean-tos of rock that had collided into each other, orange and brown again instead of gray or black, and further in the distance the green tops of trees stretching up above the rock formations. Ba said, "Only a few more hours and we back to line."

"Perfect," said Phong. We collected our water, ate the last of the protein bars, and set off again. We had one more tube of carb-gel between the three of us. It was almost over. Hope became a font of energy. I could see us emerging from this scar, standing above the earth again, surrounded by sky, smiling.

***

As we came nearer and nearer to the jungle, the scenery presented us with a view of evolution in microcosm: the carpet of vines on the floor began to bunch and knot and become bulbs of green that next bloated into knobby bushes. An hour later, trees pierced up from the bushes, thin trunks that looked like toothpicks spearing *hors d'oeurves*. The bushes here bore bundles of small flower bulbs, each with six long thin petals in the shape of almonds and bright yellow in color. The leaves around each bulb were shaped like swords and grew in clumps of about ten. The air became sticky with the sweetness of the flowers' scent. I slowed to admire them. I took a photo with my phone, eager to post it online as soon as we were high enough again to get reception. Thi had a similar flower in her bedroom growing in a clay pot that sat on her windowsill. Her flower had been white, though it had the same sword-shaped leaves on its stem, growing in threes; I had rubbed one of the petals between my fingers to see if it was real or plastic.

I felt a gentle ache in my stomach starting up. And then a sudden shiver, like a cold wind had blown softly inside of me. The warmth I felt on my skin began to fade. There was a twist in my abdomen. I didn't remember fainting. One moment, I was looking at my brother and father, all of us standing in this subterranean jungle. The next moment, I saw the trees stretching for the distant blue sky. I felt grass crushed beneath my weight and heard the hollering of my brother as a distant chirp of a voice. He was shouting, "Thanh! Oh my god, Thanh! What's wrong with him?"

On my arm, there was the grip of two strong hands pushing me over to my side as a yellow-white froth retched forward from my mouth. I writhed against the ground until I could look at both of them, could see my father crouched over me. His head was turned around, facing Phong standing a few paces away.

Ba started rattling off in Vietnamese, faster than I could keep up with in this state. He gestured wildly, a flurry of fingers. He grabbed my arm, pointed at the red rash I'd been scratching at. I recognized two words: one was enchantment and was repeated often; the other was dead. This was the way people spoke in Vietnamese though. A lot of curses had the word dead in it, so you couldn't listen to a conversation and not hear the word. Dead mother was a curse; dead sibling and dead cat and dead already and dead tomorrow and dead God too. In Vietnamese, cursing either involved something dead or something fucked.

Phong said, "I don't know, Ba."

Ba looked down at me. He spoke firmly. He asked, "Did you touch yellow flower here?"

I shook my head.

"Did you touch flower in Thi's room?"

"What?" I clutched my abdomen. I coughed up a knot of yellow-brown phlegm.

Phong tried to rush a translation. "Ba said the flower is

something called 'bạch đại ngải.' He said Thi is a thầy pháp too. The
flower's used to make antidote from its poison."

Ba barked down at me, "Cannot touch without protec-
tion!" He held my shoulder down with one hand, made a blade of
two fingers with his other that he drove hard into my lower back.
I vomited again. There was nothing but bile coming out. Ba yelled
back at Phong, "Dao!" My brother rushed over, tearing his utility
knife from his belt. Ba took it and sliced my shirt open. He drew
lines with the blade against the skin of my back. Whether I bled or
not, I couldn't say. He asked, "How long ago you touch?"

"What? I don't know." I coughed. Heat bloomed inside me.
I felt it flare up, like my stomach was a furnace. The lines on my
back were hot too; I felt like a barbecue, my back a steel grill.

Ba asked again, "How long?" He placed a flat open palm
against my stomach. He began to chant. His hand felt like ice
against the sweat on my skin.

I groaned. "I don't know, Ba," I said. "Bon. Four days," I
guessed. My heart raced, drumming the backside of my chest. The
severity of the situation fell on me like a hailstorm: I was going to
die. I was going to die because I put an ocean between myself and
my home.

Pain gurgled in my stomach. It was searing me from the
inside out, sudden sharp stabs of heat. I could feel the heat exhausting through the lines of my back, the invading coolness of
my father's hand, but it felt too slow to matter. The pain wouldn't
subside. I kept thinking about how I could come back from this,
how far away my world was. There was the cave and the river and
the forest. There was the country. There was the vast ocean. There
was my country and my state and my empty home and flowers that
wouldn't kill me. I kept grasping and grasping at something there
to hold onto, some small comfort I could bind myself to. But in
all the images of home that I conjured, I found nothing to which
I could cling. There was nothing in all the years of my life that still
brought me joy, that could remedy my suffering.

Ba spoke again. "Focus, boy. How long ago you poisoned?"

Finally, I understood what he was asking me. I called my
attention to focus. I brought my mind back from home, back to
this forest and this river and this cave. I stopped letting the pain
lead me through time, stopped pleading for it to end, stopped won-

dering when it began. I focused on the sensations of my body, my father's mystic hand cold against my belly, this poison eating me alive, the noxious wind exhausting through the slits on my back. I could feel my father's magic moving into me and out of me. And when I sat with the agony, I saw it for what it really was. I saw nothing before it and nothing after. I drew a slow breath of air and felt it too leave through my back.

I answered, "I was always poisoned."

The Grinning Man

Three weeks ago, Johnson Martin saw a black triangle in the sky while standing outside his home smoking a cigarette. It soared slowly through the air with no sound. Green and yellow lights danced along its perimeter and a white light shone from its center like a great porcelain dinner plate. Johnson Martin ran out into Main Street, finger to the heavens, screaming from deep in his belly, They're coming! They're coming! We hardly paid mind, as everyone knows that Johnson Martin is off his rocker and always spouting religious nonsense and conspiracies and the whole gamut of oddities you'd normally expect from city folk. Not long ago, we endured his Main Street sermons on the black Muslim movement storming through our town on the way to Washington, DC. He said he was trying to rally support, but Johnson Martin is one of the only blacks in our town and the other blacks—Carl Washington and his family—are wise enough to not fall in with Johnson Martin's antics. So who ever believes a thing Johnson Martin says, anyway? Besides, the very next week if you'd ask about it, he'd say, I dunno nothing bout no triangle! And then he'd spit his chew right by your feet. It'd sit there, a congealed brown mess. You'd breathe it in: the foul pungent scent of phlegm and tobacco. And then you'd walk away cause you learned better than to make conversation with Johnson Martin.

***

The Kagnan boys say they saw a strange man—at least seven feet tall by their account—through a curtain of tree trunks as they were playing in the woods. He wore green tweed-knit sports coat and had a wide, long, flat face with a broad grin sculpted into stillness that stretched to the back of his skull. The boys froze and the Grinning Man froze and they watched each other.

We hear the Grinning Man has no nose or ears; that his eyes are thin and there is too much space between them; that his flesh is hued sickly green the way Samuel Keele gets when he goes fishing. When the boys circled around him, the Grinning Man followed them with his face and nothing more. His body still, his head would turn and rotate with them as they moved. The boys heard the Grinning Man speak. He said the word cold but his lips never broke from that big grin. That was when the Kagnan boys ran, trees and branches and dirt blurring past. They looked once behind them and the Grinning Man still stood erect, unmoving, watching. And then they continued to run, as far as they could. Past the big hollowed out birch tree. Past the tree house near the Halloway place that was built for young Edgar decades ago. Past the Birchmere Farm and on and on till they got home, not once stopping for breath.

***

We paid closer attention when Brandee Birchmere started on about the Grinning Man. Such a sweet woman, no one could be more honest. Brandee says she was on her pap's farm driving the tractor to hoe up the fields for planting. She reached one end and drove in a big arc to circle back around and there he was, tall as a spruce and as wide as a stallion. His fine green jacket flapping in the wind, his smooth green face grinning ear to ear. Now, after the fact, the Kagnan boys say they think—after thinking it through—the grin was a friendly one, not so sinister as they first thought. Brandee, though, she says to us the grin was perverse and lecher-ous, with wanton lust in his spaced eyes. And what do young boys know of lust, anyway, save the filth they watch on the television these days?

She stopped the tractor and stared the man down and he stared her down, grinning all the while. Again, he never moved, not an inch, not a twitch to his lips or a blink to his eyes. Just stood and stared. Stood and stared, like he was waiting. Suddenly, the chickens began a raucous in their coops and Brandee broke her gaze. Then she says to us that when she looked back—not two seconds later—the Grinning Man was gone.

Now, we did go to check the farm, of course. All of us. And there wasn't a trace we found in that soil. No shoeprints or prints of any kind except some rabbit tracks. Later though, at Keele's Tavern, wouldn't you know that we found threads of green tweed on our boots and shoes? Then a hush fell over us and fear kept us from speaking until Edgar Halloway declared softly, Something's not right with our town these days. And then there was more silence because we knew he was right.

***

Five weeks have passed since Johnson Martin saw the black triangle, and two since the Grinning Man was seen at the Birchmere Farm. Now he was on all our minds. Who was he? Why had he come to our town? What was he doing to our folks? Billy Gardner swore up and down his wife was different. Cold, he said, like her mind had been scrubbed clean on the inside with a toothbrush. Then he said the other night, when he was leaving Keele's Tavern, he saw Old Maggie Anne talking to a tree in the woods. He crouched behind some bushes to watch and sure as April rain there was Old Maggie Anne, head crooned up to a tree.

Billy Gardner had the mind to walk the other way and take the long way home. And as he was turning, he realized that Maggie Anne wasn't speaking to a tree at all. It was the Grinning Man. So goliath that his brown slacks had been mistaken for a tree trunk. His green sports coat mistaken for leaves. The Grinning Man made eye contact with Billy and Billy says the grin stretched further to a sinister width. That was when Billy took to running.

And earlier today, someone saw Old Maggie Anne walking into the river with her clothes on. Word spread around that she went and killed herself. We wonder how lonely she was, living in that old farm with just her cat. The older of us remember when Old Maggie Anne was Maggie McIntyre, the young pride of our town. Her hair was as red and shiny as the flesh of sliced grapefruit, her frame slender; we still laugh at the way she would relentlessly flirt with Clemson Bullock—may he rest in peace—and then go out and reject his every advance.

The younger of us remember Maggie as the pretty woman who always brought chocolate milk from the McIntyre Farm with her when she babysat us. Back then we adored her.

But Clemson Bullock fell terribly ill and Maggie changed. Month by month, Clemson declined. He aged thirty years in a single one. Young taut flesh pruning into rows of wrinkles on his brow, Maggie Anne at his bedside aging right with him. By the end of it, Clemson Bullock was gone and Maggie Anne's soul evaporated in grief. She didn't speak to any of us anymore. Sold her milk and would return straight home, never a peep. Years later, she sold her cows and stopped working entirely. The McIntyre family had sixty acres of woods in our town dating back to the colonial days and she went and sold nearly all sixty to the state government. Now it's a park that city folk tourists come to camp and hunt in when they want a taste of the real world.

The idea that Old Maggie Anne—changeling or not— would walk into the river surprised not a one of us. And after Billy Gardner's story? We were expecting something of the sort. Later we saw Maggie Anne walking back from the grocery store dry as wheat. We all kept our distance. Maybe she really was Old Maggie Anne and no one had walked into the river at all, but maybe she was the changeling and made Maggie Anne go and drown herself.

***

Now, the more sensible of us are skeptics. Carl Washington went and called our town a den of fools. He says our imaginations are running from us, full sprint. That we ought to slow down and think for a second. Some of us agree, but most are growing scared. Carl Washington's words provide some comfort. They make us think we got nothing to fear from the Grinning Man. That he ain't even real. We just got an idea in our heads, that the Kagnan boys are spinning yarns and got us all spooked. We're just seeing the Grinning Man in every shadow and every tree in our town. And our town's got a whole lot of trees.

After that we feel safe and we laugh at ourselves. Carl Washington is right, after all. Den of fools.

But then a dry storm consumes the sky. Lightning snaps through the clouds. Static hangs in the air and stands the hairs on our arms and legs. When we look up, we can't help but to see forms behind the clouds, eruptions of light like raining meteors and electric orbs; we see shapes of saucers and triangles in the sky. What else are we supposed to think but the Grinning Man? He sent them here. He's one of them. And, within minutes, we all believe again cause what other proof do you need? Any fool can see they're coming, that we're under siege.

***

The sky is streams and ribbons of color. It crackles with electric booms like Chinese firecrackers in the clouds. Orbs fly, a thousand little sentient moons floating deliberately through the air. Some collide. Some zig and others zag, ravenously exploring their world. The sky draws a faint outline, a massive black triangle over our town. When we look up, we fear and are humbled. Some see doom. Others see God.

Everywhere we look, the Grinning Man is there, shadowed between trees. We see his face, still and grinning, when the lightning flashes. In anger, Billy Gardner explodes from the doors of our liquor store, shotgun in hand. We yell to him, Billy! Billy, no! Until there is a gunshot, a flash of light, and then another shot. The booms tear through the air. When the smoke and dust clears, we wait and stare at the darkness of the woods Billy Gardner shot into. When an orb spits up light from the sky, we see a tall and green and grinning figure towering and still.

We run.

All of us—half the damned town at least—push into Keele's Tavern and we board the doors. The bravest of our men gaze out the windows to see the Grinning Man and the tempest of swirling orbs of light. Our women comfort our children. To medicate the anxiety, our men drink from the taps some more.

From time to time, we see his face in a window, gazing. We wonder if he can see in the dark, see us huddling together so close. When we look away, he is gone. Samuel Keele mutters something we can't hear and then digs out a revolver and a mason jar of shine. He says, The shine's for coping. The gun's just in case. And we pass

Keele's shine around, even the women.

An hour passes. Maybe more. We hear the Grinning Man throwing rocks at the walls. The sound startles the children. It keeps us alive, wakes in each of us our fear. Stirs our anger back up with each stone that thwacks at the walls.

Edgar says, Our town is stronger than this! And he takes Billy's shotgun and blasts a shot out a window. The sound deafens us and we feel weaker, more defenseless than before. Our men get angrier. We can no longer tell who we are angry at.

Our men leap out the window, Edgar first. We think tonight that he has always been the strongest of us. Tonight we think Edgar is the greatest of us and we would lay our lives down for him. We pretend to not know Edgar sleeps with Billy Gardner's wife and that one of the Kagnan boys is his, too. We are drunk on cider and rage and terror.

Edgar fires at the trees indiscriminately. We are not sure if we can see the Grinning Man anymore. We are sure we see the Grinning Man everywhere. Up high in the tree tops. Down at our feet, buried in mud. Grins everywhere. Green everywhere. The flashes of light—of the sky and of the guns and the oil lantern someone has brought (we cannot tell who in the shadow the lantern creates)—blind us.

For hours we wander in the woods behind Edgar's lead, cheering and shooting and roaring. From time to time, the Grinning Man's face appears between trees and bushes and immediately we fire. Sometimes, his face disappears with our shots; sometimes it remains, unfazed, staring and grinning a big old grin as we run riotously away. Even the Kagnan boys are with us. One of them points and says, Look! Down the trail!

We see it. His shadow is enormous. He stands centered on the trail, broad and dark and still. We freeze in shock. The longer we stare, the more mammoth he becomes. It is dark, but we swear his grin glows faintly. He shifts his weight and Edgar roars, He's brought them! They're coming for us now, don't none of you dare let him get away! And we roar with Edgar. The Grinning Man runs away from us, his shadow shrinking in the distance until we chase after. There is so much noise we hardly hear anything but ourselves. Then there is another boom—our boom. And the figure falls.

Edgar reaches it first. We prod at the body as we wait for

light. The man with the light is far behind. Someone says, Looks awfully small!

No! shouts another. That's it! The Grinning Man! I've seen it!

Johnson Martin belts, We have killed the menace! We will be free!

When the light comes, we crouch to the body. And then we turn away as something somersaults in our stomach and we feel ill.

Someone whispers, Old Maggie Anne. We killed her.

Someone else argues, She was one of them! Don't you remember?

We shoot accusatory glances at one another. We wonder: who fired? Edgar with the shotgun or Keele with his revolver? Many of us hold firearms. We remember gripping the handles in white-knuckled vices. We remember our fear and outrage. When we look up and gaze through the canopies at the swirling lights above, the guttural rumbles of the sky, we don't know what we're looking at anymore.

Edgar is silent. He lifts Maggie Anne into his arms. Come on, he says soberly. Let's go back.

We follow.

It is quiet as we return, the gnawing sort of silence, the silence of sound. Insects buzz, birds call, thunder rolls, our boots *clop-clop* against the packed dirt beneath us. Its rhythm beats our shame into us. When we are back on Main Street, we see Carl Washington approach. He asks, What the hell happened?

Someone yells, The sky! The Grinning Man brought them!

We realize how absurd it sounds.

Carl shakes his head. He spits out, Damned fools, the lot of you. And look who had to pay. Watch the news sometime and stop sipping Keele's shine all day. And then Carl Washington walks on and away.

We look at each other, bewildered, ashamed, certain and uncertain all at once of what transpired and what we saw. We talk amongst ourselves while we deliver Maggie Anne to the hospital. Edgar stays with her and we talk back at Keele's too. Our women confirm the Grinning Man's face leering in through the windows and the thrown stones. Our men remember the Grinning Man standing in the woods, his body a skyscraper over Old Maggie Anne. We remember how he dragged her deeper into the wood and how she screamed at us for help and how Edgar dove ahead and fired at the Grinning Man, scaring him off. And when we looked down to retrieve Maggie Anne, we noticed then that stray pellets had struck her. We pass the story amongst ourselves until we are sure of every last detail, until we have wrung it of every drip of truth. And then we drink.

Prophecy

Anna has spent a minimum of seventy-three hours a month in Dr. Samson's office for the past six years. She did the math once in a waiting room. Ever since Colin was diagnosed, Anna has lived part of her life breathing in the piercing stench of sterility, the sting of medical disinfectant. Now she is listening to Dr. Samson explain the latest blood results. It sounds the same as the last time.

"His creatinine levels are elevated," the doctor says.

Anna asks, "What does that mean?"

"We don't know," he says.

It's always 'we' when there's a problem. Colin doesn't have a team of doctors, not most of the time. Still, Dr. Samson insists on 'we,' as if the nurses and receptionists in their spaced-out uninvolved little worlds had anything to do with the blood work. Oh, the nurse Sera jammed the needle in and maybe Sue at the desk filed the results in the right folder—good for her!—but that doesn't mean it isn't Dr. Samson alone who 'doesn't know.'

It's impossible for Anna not to hate Dr. Samson. She should love him for all that he does, for as long he has been there for Colin, but there is a deep chasm between those words—'*should*' and '*love*'.

The sight of Dr. Samson's thick gray moustache churns butter in her stomach. When she sleeps, his voice resonates in her dreams like a devil on her shoulder. Except instead of temptations Dr. Samson whispers medical tests and procedures. When Anna wakes every morning, she immediately checks on Colin, immediately curses the doctor for lying to her, immediately feels a pang of guilt for her anger.

The doctor pauses. Anna must have been glaring, so she takes deep breaths to cool the fire from her eyes. "Well, there's a chance his kidneys haven't been processing the creatinine. His urine has a pretty high level, too. And some blood."

"There's damage," she says, not liking how he said the word '*chance*'.

Dr. Samson's eyes dart away.

"It's reversible, right?" Anna asks.

"We don't know yet," he answers.

"The Remicade," she says, remembering. Colin had been on it to treat the Crohn's, but Dr. Samson took him off it last year. His creatinine levels had been too high and the doctor suspected the Remicade was responsible.

He runs a thumb down the file in his hand like there might be something there, something new and different from before. Finally the doctor replies, "If the Remicade was causing the issues, then it was only part of it. We're going to set up an appointment with a renal specialist. He'll take more blood, and maybe we can examine the kidneys." Anna doesn't hide her glare anymore. She vents. "You're not going to tell me, on top of the Crohn's, on top of being sick for half of his damned life, he might have to deal with kidney failure?"

"No," the doctor says. "I'm not going to tell you that. We'll figure it all out. Until then, I'll pray for you."

Anna doesn't ask why he would pray for her instead of Colin. She is the one who needs God's forgiveness.

***

The autumn comes as a relief for Anna. The humidity that suffocated her in the summer months gives way to a blissful chill. The leaves lose life and they are reborn in bright and vibrant colors. All the best family events happen in the autumn: apple-picking, the renaissance fair, discount ticket prices at amusement parks. In these brief months, when life whimpers down, before all is snuffed by the heartless sterile snow, Anna believes in God and herself and Colin. Again, if briefly.

This weekend, Anna and Joseph take Colin apple-picking.

The colors of autumn collide in the orchard—there are reds and pinks, yellows and oranges, greens and golds in leaves and apples. The scent of spice, wood and smoke hang in the air, accented by the frosty chill stinging her nose with each breath. Colin runs off ahead, his legs beating the ground, a harsh and clumsy stomp in his short strides. Anna's husband, Joseph, chases after, roaring the way fathers do. Anna has never understood the monster-play between men and boys, but she remembers how her own father would roar monstrously at her brother. Somehow it's endearing.

They are waiting. Anna expects a call any time. Within the hour, if she's lucky. Three days if she's not. Colin has been a scheduled for surgery next week; the call will just confirm it. Anna doesn't like the idea. She imagines her boy on the table, splayed open while white-cloaked masked men dig and prod.

"They're gonna open me up," explains Colin to Joseph excitedly.

Joseph asks, "Oh yeah? What're they going to do that for?"

Colin says, "I have a problem with my kiddies."

Joseph laughs. "Kidneys," he corrects.

"I have a problem with my kidneys," repeats Colin. "And the doctors are going to go inside me and fix it!"

Colin starts up a small tree barely taller than Joseph. He calls down, "Mom! Dad! Watch this!"

And then he scurries into the canopy and vigorously shakes a branch until applies, like a volley of golden-green tennis balls, rain down to the earth.

Joseph laughs again. "Wow," he says. "You're pretty strong. Bet a strong guy like you isn't afraid of the doctors, huh?"

"Nope," says Colin cheerfully. "They don't scare me."

Anna looks away.

***

Today he was supposed to have the surgery. Everything had been prepared and maybe the doctors could finally figure out what was wrong. But yesterday, Anna's phone had rung and the nurse had talked about a new appointment and a different doctor. Platelets, the nurse had said. Something about platelets, though Anna cannot remember. It is hard for her to recall these details, even as she tries to glue every word she hears to her mind.

She wants Colin to live a normal life without the daily blinding white of linoleum and fluorescence bearing into his and her skin. Colin had missed sixty days of school last year. Sixty! That was more than a third!

Now she drives him to the new doctor. A hematologist. A *blood* specialist. It sounds ugly to her. It sounds visceral and Anna doesn't like the thought of her boy being cut up to begin with, but that's life for her now. It's a choice between life skinned open or death and she will not lose Colin, not to this or the kidney thing or the Crohn's.

It was a ridiculous genetic gamble. There are over thirty separate genes that have been shown to link to Crohn's disease and the random hodge-podge of her twenty-three chromosomes and Joseph's twenty-three chromosomes somehow—magically— turned all thirty of those individual genes to '*On*.' She cries herself to sleep most nights, praying and praying and praying to God that it all be undone. Let Colin be healthy, she begs. Let him go to school. Let him be able to play outside. Let him have a real life.

Every morning, she awakens to find God has haplessly ig- nored her pleas. The clouds still swirl in the sky and, from time to time, obscure the sun and cast the world into the drab of gray and rain and snow. She looks at her hands every day and sees they plump through time and she dares not look at her stomach. It is too much already to feel the strain of her shirts against her abdo- men. She is angry and rueful at God's callous betrayal until she remembers her place and apologizes, holding the cross around her neck to her forehead.

***

The hematologist is named Skinner. The name tastes foul in her mouth and she doesn't like the impression it leaves in her mind, red and hot like a brand. It reminds Anna of what they want to do. *Skin* Colin. Split him open and poke and prod and see if moving this tube over that way might fix the problem. Or maybe they'll just inject some clear liquid—more vodka-like than water-like—into the gray-brown legume of his kidney and it will be like magic or poison or nothing.

"His blood isn't clotting," Dr. Skinner explains to her. "We don't know how, or if, he'd recover if he turns out to be hemophiliac."

"We get his blood tested *every* month," Anna shouts angrily. "Why can't you *tell?*"

The doctor, graying hair and wrinkles wrapped up in a white coat like a clone of the others, shakes his head. "No," he says. "Dr. Samson hasn't tested for it before. It's a whole different sort of procedure. Tell me, does Colin get a lot of nosebleeds?"

"Well, yeah, he gets nosebleeds. All kids do."

"Maybe it's nothing," the doctor responds. "The nosebleeds, I mean. But let me take a moment to explain. Colin could have one of two things. The first is hemophilia, the one everyone knows. Hemophilia is carried in the X chromosome and, like most other X-related conditions, is overwhelmingly represented by males. Women have two Xs, so they have a higher likelihood of just being carriers. The dominant and healthy X will always compensate, so women rarely inherit the disease."

It sounds like gibberish to Anna. She catches onto one important thing, probably what Dr. Skinner is getting at as politely as he can: it is her fault, her genes and not Joseph's that have imparted this calamity upon Colin. She understands genetics enough to know that. In the case of a boy, the father only contributes a Y.

"The other possibility is von Willebrand Disease," continues Dr. Skinner, oblivious to the sudden streak of guilt that mars Anna's face.

Truth be told, the stain of guilt and the stain of stress on one's face are nearly indistinguishable. No matter what, Anna always looks haggard these days. There is darkness pooling beneath her eyes and crow's feet clawing deeper beside them, ready to claim her face. Her cheeks have swollen round so that she is self-conscious in Chinese restaurants, paranoid that the patrons and staff all compare her to the jolly golden Budai laughing and rubbing his globular belly by the door. She will take it, though. The weight, the stress, the guilt, if Colin might someday get better. So she listens to Dr. Skinner intently, even though she imagines he is jeering internally, criticizing her stomach's circumference and her intelligence and her ability to mother a boy like Colin.

"Von Willebrand Disease is carried in chromosome 12,"

Dr. Skinner continues to explain.

Suddenly, Anna cannot hold onto the doctor's words. She catches *platelets* and something about factors. *Lacking factor seven,* he says on two different occasions. And then he says *eight* and *nine* and Anna doesn't know what the words mean. She thinks they must be important, because he has said the words so often.

Dr. Skinner pauses for a moment. And then he asks, "Does that make some sense?"

Anna nods, although it is still senseless babble to her. She will do her own research later. She will read until her eyes are red and Joseph tries to bribe her into bed or just unplug the computer because *he's* had enough. When she wakes up, she will read again. And again and again. She will read until every last word, acronym, and Roman numeral has seared itself into the folds of her brain.

***

When Joseph comes home from work, Anna is reading at the computer. She stops to tell him what Dr. Skinner said. Joseph finds the couch and turns the TV on.

"He'll be fine," says Joseph. "Either way, it can be treated, right? And I bet it's neither, anyhow."

Men are stupid, Anna decides. They don't like doctors, so they don't go until the last crucial second. Men think that everything will be okay. Until it isn't and there is nothing left but fear.

Anna exclaims angrily, "He doesn't need this on top of everything else. He's already facing renal disease! His medical record is already thicker than your dissertation!"

"He'll be fine," repeats Joseph, this time slower as if that meant Anna would believe him now. She instead wonders why people think that saying something slower than the first time changes anything. She is nothing but anger now.

But then Joseph stands. He comes to her and places a hand on her shoulder, looking down with eyes welled with just enough water to let Anna know he is fighting tears. Joseph says, "It's just a biopsy, Anna. Nothing serious."

She wants to say that Colin is just a boy, but she hears what Joseph is saying and she nods. Her hand finds his and squeezes gently. Anna relaxes underneath his touch. She is amazed at how relieving it is to have Joseph's strength.

***

Anna has a personal trainer she sees twice a week. It is as much for weight control (she no longer deludes herself into thinking that she can *lose* weight) as it is for stress relief. She also talks to him about Colin, about Joseph, about Dr. Samson and all manner of other things. She has cried in front of him twice. She understands what *physical therapy* means now.

It is Thursday morning after seeing Dr. Skinner and taking (another) blood sample from Colin. She repeats her words to Joseph to the young boy, Michael, paid to listen and torture her with movements that she hates so that she forgets everything else she hates. She sees herself and the boy a thousand times over, reflected in the mirrors multiplying tunnel visions of bodies and muscle and metal ad infinitum. The machines are painted white, but the barbells are ancient. They are colored like slate and each has a red-brown dusting of rust that always stains her hands and clothes orange. Michael doesn't know how to respond, so he makes a face and bows his head silently. When he speaks at last, he says, "That's a pretty stacked medical record."

"I know," Anna replies, appreciating the effort if nothing else. "Poor kid."

Michael, uncertain of what to say next, falls to silence and demonstrates a full squat, holding a large dumbbell to his chest. Immediately after rising, he hands it to Anna and she takes it clumsily. It looked so much smaller in his hands. It looks now like it has magically grown a quarter-size and Anna thinks of Wonderland.

***

Three years ago, in the stifling white sterility of Dr. Samson's office, Anna asked: "Why Colin? Why is this happening?"

Dr. Samson pushed his eyeglasses up the bridge of his nose with a single finger, leaned back in his seat and gazed out of his office window without saying anything. The sky was a field of clouds and after the January snow, you could never tell where earth stopped and the heavens began. The white sickened Anna that day.

She was tired of it. Her eyes had given up on white and settled on a gentler color more pink than red.

"You know," started Dr. Samson, "the main issue a lot of people have with evolution—other than the whole religion thing, of course—is that it is too reliant on *random mutation* and we can't account for the random. In some ways, it doesn't make sense."

He said this next part in a hushed voice, like it was a guarded secret: *"But neither does quantum mechanics."*

He belly-laughed and Anna felt a short surge of guilt because she hadn't realized it was a joke.

He continued, "The thing is that if there truly is *random* genetic mutation, without cause, then we can't predict anything in genetics. Trends wouldn't exist. It would mean that disease—any disease—could spring up at any time in any one. But that's not the case, is it? Conditions arise out of genetic prophecy. There's no such thing as random chance, just varying degrees of probability. And when it comes right down to it, we can be fairly certain of most outcomes if we know two people's genetic codes."

He began to idly drum the back of his pen into his desk and he still peered out the window without once looking at Anna. His upper lip was beaded with sweat, clinging as tiny crystal balls to each individual pillar of stubble composing his shadowed beard.

Dr. Samson went on, "If I were to guess, I'd say that the scientists just say it so other people don't get to blaming themselves. I don't know if knowing would change anything or if it would change everything."

He shrugged. "But, hey, even if it's written in blood doesn't mean it's fatalistic, you know?"

***

Colin is thin. His ribs are like the stretched-out bellows of an accordion, stacked neatly. Joseph tells her that all boys are skinny and Colin will fatten up with age. She sees fat boys all the time, though, and doesn't believe Joseph.

When Colin naps, Anna sometimes sits in his room, reading quietly. She doesn't know why she needs to be near him at these times. Now, she puts her book down and touches his face. The hillock of his cheek depresses at her fingertips. Surprise takes her.

For a moment, she expected his cheek to dissolve into dust at her touch. For a moment, she thought her boy was *papier-mâché*.

"Mom," he asks with as much rasp as a boy's voice can muster, in his gentle croaking voice of first awakening.

"*Shh*," replies Anna. "I'm here, Colin."

He turns his face into the pillow. Or maybe he is shaking his head.

"You worry too much, Mom," says Colin when his face emerges, facing the other way. Away from her. She touches his hair, tousling it as if it were still as long as last year. She remembers how it felt like silk thread slipping between her fingers. Cropped short, it is still soft, like fur. She knows one day it will feel like dry bristles the way Joseph's does. One day, the years will take their toll and the silk will give way to straw.

The doctors' visits and hospital trips never bother Colin. He rarely whines or cries or mopes. He goes and he gives them blood and he pees into a cup and he lets them gouge at his body with silver prods and electrode patches. Sometimes, he giggles and says, "Look, Mom! I'm a robot!" And then he makes *whoosh* sound effects when he's all strapped in. Anna feels her heart plummet at those moments, because he knows no other life, until she starts to wonder if he does know and if he is being strong.

And then Anna decides she's better off not knowing.

***

When Anna returns from the grocery store, she sees a voicemail on her phone and a missed call from Dr. Skinner's office. Dread and anxiety both settle into the depths of her stomach and she throws the phone back into her purse, hangs it on a coat hook by the door and then walks away. It is hours before she returns to it and only by necessity because it rings. Colin's school is calling.

The moment Anna arrives in the nurse's office, she sees Colin sitting in the corner, hugging his knees and casting his eyes down. The nurse says to her, "He's been in and out of the bathroom. I don't think it's very pleasant."

Anna kneels by Colin. "Hey," she says. "What's going on?"

"It hurts," Colin murmurs.

"Is it your stomach?"

Colin shakes his head. "No, it hurts to pee," says Colin.

Anna sighs. "Come on," she says. "Let's go home. You'll be more comfortable."

When the nurse prepares the paperwork for Colin's dismissal, Anna listens to her voicemail. She first hears Dr. Skinner clear his throat. The sound clips into a harsh static and Anna has to pull the phone away for a second.

"Hello, Anna?" Dr. Skinner starts. "This is Dr. Skinner. The results of the blood work have come back. I honestly cannot find anything abnormal in his blood. We think the previous sample must have been contaminated or just a momentary halt in production. He's been cleared for the kidney biopsy, but I would like to continue monitoring his blood once a month for lacking factors. I've already arranged this with Dr. Samson, so this will be of no trouble to you. Dr. Samson will take charge and just add another test in to the routine blood work, a small blip on the insurance. Thank you and I hope Colin recovers well."

The anger erupts through her veins in boiling blood. Anger and relief, but mostly anger. Begrudgingly, she will call and schedule the biopsy when Colin and her return home.

***

Joseph is distracted. The waiting room is cacophonous in that silent sort of way, a causal orchestra of shuffling papers, random beeps, automatic doors sliding open and shut, wheelchairs rolling and the percussion of hundreds of feet beating linoleum tile. Colin is open somewhere on a table. It takes all her energy to not envision it, not picture what they might be doing in there to her boy. She focuses instead on Joseph and knows right away his mind on his something else entirely. Anna knows his moods from the rhythm of his breaths. Right now, the inhales are long and there's a deep pause before a short and powerful exhale. The staccato of his breath means that something is bothering him, but he doesn't know how to actually feel about it. She also knows that he does not know whether he wants Anna to ask him what is wrong. She does anyway, because he normally wants her to. When she asks, he blinks twice quickly and then looks at her. His thick brown brows are pressed together. He looks sad, almost. He says to her,

"Nothing. It's just some things at work are on my mind."

Anna scowls. "You're thinking about work right now?"

"It's a biopsy, Anna," says Joseph. "They're just trying to figure out what's going on. Nothing's going to happen to him."

Anna casts her eyes to the ground. She asks, "What's with that look?"

He asks, "What look?"

"Something's on your mind."

Joseph shakes his head. "It's nothing," he says.

She doesn't respond to him. She just makes an impatient face until he caves. It is a skill Anna has perfected over many years.

Finally, he relents and says, "It just disappoints me that you've stopped believing in God."

"What? What has that to do with anything? And what do you mean? Of course I believe in God!"

Anna huffs with frustration and turns away from her husband.

Joseph's voice is calm and tinged with disappointment. The sound of it clutches Anna's heart and she tries not to cry, though her throat has dried and the stolen moisture creeps to her eyes anyway. He says to her, "I don't mean in that way. I mean you have no faith in God. You've stopped believing that he will do right in this world. You've stopped believing in his love. You've stopped believing in your love for God, too."

Anna says nothing. She wipes her eyes and stops breathing, as if stopping her breaths might halt the tears.

"I know I'm right," says Joseph. "But I'm not asking you to believe in God. I don't think that matters. I want you to believe in Colin. I want you to believe in his strength and that he will be okay."

She turns to her husband. "What makes you think I don't believe in him?"

"Because you don't."

Joseph reaches out and touches her arm.

He says, "You don't believe in our son as a person. As a human being. All you see is the disease. Do you even know him? What's his favorite color?" Anna says nothing. Joseph says, "Yellow. What's his favorite superhero?"

"Batman," says Anna.

"Mr. Incredible," corrects Joseph. "What's his favorite video game?"

"I don't know! The one with the guns."

Joseph laughs and the antagonism is momentarily suspended. "No, that's *my* favorite video game. His is Zelda. The one with the elf-boy and the sword."

Now he sighs and Anna feels the tension escalate again.

"Get to know our son, Anna. He's an actual person. For all his youth, he knows what's going on. And he's okay with it. You need to believe in him too. If his mother can't have faith in him, then he's lost."

Joseph reaches for her and Anna jumps at the sudden cold of his fingers, but she sighs and submits and is pulled into his arms and against his chest. Joseph whispers into her ear now.

"I'm sorry," he says. "We need to be strong. For Colin. We need to have faith."

Anna looks away again. She pulls herself away from Joseph and then falls into a chair. The fabric is itchy and wool-like and the cushion gives too quickly to the wood beneath. She buries her hands in her face. Her mind races through everything she knows about her son. Blood type A-negative. Seventy-eight pounds. Four-foot nine inches. Crohn's. Creatinine clearance, forty milliliters a minute. School days missed last year, sixty-three. Favorite movie? Book? Food?

Joseph sits next to her, drapes an arm around her, leans in and kisses her cheek. Anna stares at the floor tiles.

***

It has been six weeks. Colin has been released from the hospital. They found several holes in his kidneys, like a million microscopic pellets had ravaged the organs. A wave of piercing particles like some violent double-slit experiment. Still, the surgeons called it *acute* renal disease. When the report reached back to Dr. Samson, he declared, "Colin will be able to live as normal a life as a boy can with Crohn's. We can put him on some steroids temporarily and that should restore his creatinine levels. He'll have renal disease for the rest of his life but it might never be a problem."

Anna had shaken her head to this. "Or it might be a problem," she said.

Dr. Samson replied, "Yes, there's always a chance. But it's unlikely, now that we know."

Anna nodded and silently thanked God. She'd gone to church every Sunday since. She will go next Sunday, too.

Now, they are at the renaissance fair that comes for the autumn months. Deep-fryers sizzle in the distance, coating absurdities like Twinkies and Oreos in crisped fat. Swords cling and clang. Women are dressed in corsets of elaborate colors—pink like sea foam, or forest moss green, or the pale blue of jay feathers. Men in leather jerkins are adorned with claymores at their hips.

Anna stops at a wooden booth displaying rows of ornate jewelry on red velvet. She picks up a necklace, spreading the chain between her spread index and middle fingers. An oval pendant, inlayed with a ruby, gently swings as she brings it up to Joseph's eye. "This is nice, isn't it?"

Joseph laughs and takes the pendant in his hand. "All right, all right," he says.

"Mom, if you get that, can I get a sword?" Colin asks.

Anna says, "They're really expensive."

Joseph says, "He probably means a toy one, Anna."

Colin chimes in, "A toy's fine. I meant a real one, though."

Joseph points his finger. "You can have a real one if you pull the sword out of the stone there."

Colin rushes toward it excitedly.

Anna asks, "What are you doing? What if he can pull it?"

Joseph shrugs. "Then I get a new sword."

There is a line for the sword in the stone. It is an attraction and there is a display of trinkets for prizes to successful participants. Anna sees a woman approach, wrap her slender fingers with both hands around the hilt and begin her efforts. She is dressed the way female warriors are depicted in medieval movies, a corset of dark brown leather with a deep square-cut. Her breasts hang low and bounce with her efforts and Anna watches the line of men—and Joseph—lean in and gawk. Anna slaps her husband.

"What? You can't blame me. They're there! You stared, too. Admit it."

Joseph laughs.

Anna rolls her eyes. The woman didn't manage to budge

the sword. A series of men follow, some sliding the sword halfway out, some failing worse somehow than the woman, and only one freeing the sword. The crowd roars in applause and the man, who looks more like a recreational bodybuilder than a recreational table-top gamer, bows and smiles and waves. He replaces the sword, takes his trinket, and begins to try and talk to the woman from before. No doubt, he thinks his machismo might win her over. She immediately walks away and Anna chuckles.

Colin is next. He walks up to the sword and paces to each side of it three times. The sun catches his eyes, illuminates their chocolate brown, as he scans it. He is too short to pull the sword like the adults have tried. The butt of the hilt is at his solar plexus when he walks up to it. Next, he looks at his own hands and Anna imagines he is thinking to himself, How wiry! How weak I am!

Colin turns around.

Joseph touches Anna's arm. "See? Nothing to worry about. He can't even try."

But then Colin beams and grins ear to ear, stepping backward until his back hits the blade. He lowers himself, grasping the cross-guard with his hands and pulling it into his upper back. His tiny face goes bright red and Anna sees his hips and knees open.

She gasps. "He's trying to squat the sword up."

Joseph cranes his head forward. "What? Do you think he'll get it? No, no, he won't get it."

The sword moves upward and the crowd begins to cheer and holler and clap their hands fervently. Anna sees tears rolling down Colin's cheek, sees all the strain he is putting into the effort. The sword is halfway freed, but Colin is slowing. He digs his feet hard into the stone beneath him, but the sword rises only inch by inch and Colin is losing his breath.

Joseph says again, "Do you think he'll get it? This is insane! He's got to be out of energy by now. He won't get it."

Anna says, "He'll get it."

Beware of Dogma

Kesuk leads a small hunting team into the wilds. They ride four kayaks—one person and three dogs each—across a thin ribbon of ocean from the town to the ice. The terrain is mostly flat, though the wind has carved dunes in the snow that cast curving stripes of shadow on the landscape. In the distance, glaciers form a faintly blue fence.

Each winter, communities of spotted seals and walruses climb onto floating icicle islands in the Arctic Ring. The islands then converge and the scars of dark water between them seal up solid. This means the bears are also out, bears that are starved from summer, eager to feast on the new winter life scattered over the ice.

In the place of other Inuits, there is a camera crew—two thin white men, one plump black woman. A documentary for some educational television series. The mayor insisted. Kesuk argued that it was bad luck, that these outsiders hadn't performed the rituals and Nanook would be angry. The bears would avoid them. But the mayor said the film would bring tourists and tax dollars, that their lives would be much better off long term.

The white man in charge is called Mark, a thin and mousy man with cropped hair the color of aged ivory. He wears a black down jacket that poofs only subtly, rather than layers of furs. The other man is named Chad. He looks younger than Mark and is the tallest. He handles the camera, which is smaller than Kesuk can remember cameras looking, no larger than a tin lunchbox. When, he wonders, did cameras get so small? Chad the cameraman wears manufactured clothes too. Kesuk placed a bet with the mayor on how long the white men will last on the ice. He is pretty sure he will win.

The black woman is named Yolanda; she is well-liked. She is fat and beautiful; she does not call Kesuk or the other Inuits *eskimos*. When they met, she asked about the *amautiit* the women wear, warm throws of hide and fur with a fat pouch to carry a child or supplies. They gave her one made of sealskin. Immediately, she pulled the parka over her head and shoulders. She has worn it since. The *amautiit* once appeared of a similar complexion to tree bark; the leather has lost this shade after so many years of having braved the harsh blades of winter sunlight, and now appears the color of soft cream. The contrast against the deep brownness of Yolanda's skin makes her hue appear richer to Kesuk, as if she had been painted with sweet dark syrup, something he could drink up.

Kesuk ties the kayaks to stakes he has hammered into the ice. Mark is standing behind him, watching over his shoulders. "Everything looks the same out here," says Mark. "How do you know how to get back?"

"The dogs know," answers Kesuk. He turns and looks at Mark. He points at the sky. "The stars, too."

"Oh, awesome. We'll make sure to get some shots of you reading the stars."

"Great," says Kesuk. He imagines, for just a moment, thrusting a spear into Mark's soft white belly. But it would be unsatisfying. The man has no meat. And what flesh actually does cling to his bones probably tastes like fast food hamburgers. And the rest of the town will notice. And the camera probably makes murder a little too messy.

"What're you smiling at?" asks Mark. He bounces on the balls of his feet and wraps himself in his arms. "It's freezing out here. Don't know how you can stand it."

Kesuk shakes his head. He flicks the lines tethering the kayaks to ice. "Inuits always smile."

Mark points to Chad, who is screwing his camera onto a tripod in the ice. "Can we get a shot of you tying the kayaks up?"

Kesuk sighs. Chad says, "Just a few more minutes. It's hard to get the lighting right with all this snow." He says he has to play with the *filters*, although all he does is press buttons. He raises a pistoled hand and flicks his wrist down in a mock firing at Kesuk.

It's taken twenty-five minutes to set up the shot. Kesuk has stayed in his squat for the duration. The kayaks clap together on occasion behind him. Mark hovers over his shoulder, ready to narrate to the camera how Kesuk ties the kayak. And, after that, how he rigs the dog sleds up. Kesuk feels the muscles in his forearms twitching. Mark should be rigging his own sled; they'd spent two days alone teaching the crew how.

Kesuk straps a rifle into his sled. He recalls, briefly, when his father first gave him the gun, his first hunt at fifteen, his first kill at nineteen. He looks away, at the mainlanders filming him.

Yolanda stands between Kesuk and the camera, out of shot. She asks, "Can you tell us a little about your hunting procedures?"

Kesuk nods. He fusses with his hood. It keeps nudging the microphone clipped to his shirt collar out of place. "Federal regulation prohibits us from killing more than five hundred bears a year between the Inuit populations of the US and Canada. Our town has three tags, so that's up to three kills if we're lucky. We have two with us today, but we shouldn't expect to use any."

"So what happens if you kill more polar bears than you have tags for?"

He shrugs his shoulders and laughs. "If you try to sell it, you will probably be put in federal prison for a very long time."

"Oh," says Yolanda. She straightens her posture. "So you could technically just kill a bear and leave it out here? Like, there's nothing stopping someone from just hunting for sport?"

"If you're okay with being a horrible person," answers Kesuk.

"Cut, cut, cut," says Mark, speeding across the snow from the sleds. "Can you repeat the same thing in your language? We can add subtitles over it."

Kesuk thins his eyes. "I speak English just fine."

"Well, how about in a thicker accent?" Mark smiles. "The audience might be uncomfortable with how good your English is. They won't believe you're what you say you are."

"That's ridiculous." Kesuk stands and squats back down three times. He shakes his legs loose. "And can we hurry this up? We're wasting time."

"Look, this is television. Nobody expects authenticity. They expect someone less American. More tribal, you know? So, how about that accent?" Mark nods enthusiastically, still smiling, agreeing with his own suggestion.

Kesuk looks at Yolanda. Her face darkens and she looks away for a moment. She says, "It will probably increase ratings."

"Fine," he replies. He begins to make sounds with his throat. Dog-like. The calls of beasts. The sounds mean nothing. The Inuits will laugh at this when they see it. Kesuk decides to gesture with his hands too, using them to illustrate a tale of Mark being bludgeoned by a bear's femur later in the trip. He walks his right hand to his left. He makes a fist, slamming it into his open palm repeatedly. And then he smiles at Mark, showing his teeth, and nods in the same enthused manner as Mark had just moments ago.

"Perfect!" exclaims Mark.

"Okay, we are done," says Kesuk, walking back to the sleds. "We have a lot of land to cover." He catches Yolanda covering her mouth with both hands, her cheeks rounded and her eyes squinted. Their eyes meet for a moment. She looks away immediately. One breath of laughter escapes unstifled. The woman is smart, Kesuk notes. Maybe Nanook will favor this hunt after all.

***

There are three sleds instead of two. The third is steered by Chad, who has his camera harnessed to his chest. He can nudge it with his hands, pointing the lens at the other sleds or at empty scenery whizzing by. His sled alternates between following behind Kesuk—who is accompanied by Yolanda—and following behind Mark. The running dogs kick up flakes of frost into the air. All Kesuk hears is the sound of their panting. And Yolanda's voice. She exclaims, "I never imagined that dogs could move this fast."

Kesuk scans the horizon. The distant glaciers blur into the blue of the sky and the white of the clouds. There are only the colors of ice, of steel, of sea and ash. He looks for an interruption in the pattern, a point where the curving shadows striping the snow divot, where paws or bellies might have bowled through the windblown white.

There. In the distance. An ellipsis of darkness. A long string of shadow stuttering where the crest of snow has been stepped through.

He waves his arm in the air and then speeds after his sighting. If the white men can't figure out to follow, he has a good story mapped in his mind to explain their deaths.

When Kesuk arrives at the patch of broken snow, pride balloons in his belly. Bear prints punch a trail through the sea ice, winding off beyond the end of sight. He hops off his sled. He kneels beside a paw print, examines its edges for a hardened crust of frost. Yolanda steps up behind him. She says, "Turn your microphone on." He groans, but reaches for the device clipped to his belt. She asks, "Can you tell us what you're looking for?"

Kesuk draws his finger in the air along the perimeter of the print. "This edge will freeze first. The print is still fresh powder. If this was a windier day, I'd say that we'd be in good shape. The trail could be as little as an hour old." He looks out over the expanse of white and gray. "But the wind has little strength this winter; the tracks could be hours old, but no more than three. The prints would have begun to freeze over already."

"As much as three hours?" she repeats. "Is that good or bad?"

He shrugs his shoulders. "Not bad. On the sleds, it shouldn't be more than half that time to catch up to the bear."

The baying of the hounds announces the arrival of the others. Kesuk looks over at Mark and Chad stepping off their sleds, waddle-running through the snow.

"So what now?" asks Mark. He bends over and dusts the snow off his knees and thighs.

Chad has his lens zoomed in on the tracks. Yolanda is kneeling in the snow by a paw print, regurgitating Kesuk's words to the camera. Why did she have him turn his microphone on if she was going to say the same thing? Chad pans up to reveal the trail. The tracks create a visibly raised line of snow that weaves off into the horizon.

Kesuk says, "We follow the tracks on sled. See if we can't catch up to the bear."

Yolanda turns to the Inuits. "Some of these prints look like human feet," she says.

Kesuk laughs. "Have you ever seen the bottom of a bear's foot before?" Everyone stares. He laughs again, this time quieter. His cheeks warm. "Oh. Well, their hind paws look the same as ours. Except they have claws."

Chad points at the paw print beside Yolanda. "Yeah! I heard something about these scientists who think the Yeti is some ancient polar bear relative. You think Sasquatch might be a polar bear too?"

Kesuk leans forward. He places a hand on Chad's shoulder and says softly, "Sasquatch is real. And has brown hair." He turns toward Mark next, points a finger back at the sled. "You can fire a rifle, right? There's one sheathed at your side."

Mark blinks, dumbfounded. "From a moving sled?"

"No," he answers. "You stop first. Now get back on your sleds. We waste too much time getting on and off like this for your damned movie."

When they are riding again, Yolanda asks into Kesuk's ear, "Do you actually believe in Sasquatch?"

"We don't have Sasquatch in Alaska. Why wouldn't I?"

"Well, I mean, science."

Kesuk laughs. He feels how it jostles her, how she pastes her chest to his back for stability. "Scientists come here all the time. We like scientists. I did my undergrad in biology in Juno."

"Oh," she says. "So why do you believe in Sasquatch?"

He shrugs.

"But how could a creature that large possibly evade science for so long?" Kesuk laughs again. He turns his head and meets her eyes. "What are you doing? Keep your eyes on the snow!"

He doesn't turn his head. He closes his eyes with a grin. "This really bothers you, doesn't it?"

"Which part?"

He opens his eyes and looks ahead again, still chuckling. "Sasquatch."

"Yes, it does."

"I said we like scientists, right?" She hums an affirmative into his ear. He takes a minute to think. How can he explain this? "The reason is because they don't have these notions of what is real and what is not, only what can and cannot be tested. They tell us all the time that the world cannot actually speak to us, but all they can say for sure is that we always find exactly what we are looking for, even if it's a rare flower buried beneath this snow. They can't tell us we're wrong, because we always find it. We'll find this bear too, because it wants to be found."

She is quiet. The fur of her hood brushes against the back of his as she gently nods her head. "But people are looking for Bigfoot all the time."

He shrugs his shoulders. "All I mean is that science has no dogma. It requires accepting that we're already wrong."

Yolanda's hand is fumbling around his waist. He feels a click. She turned his microphone on. "What do you mean when you say the polar bear will let you find it?"

"We believe that all things have souls. People, bears, dogs, sleds, guns, tools. Our people exist only through consuming souls, using souls, ending souls."

"So the bears have souls. Okay." Her nods are slow. "Why would it let itself die?"

Kesuk says over his shoulder, "Because we offer the souls of our tools to them in the afterlife."

"And what if you're wrong? What if the bear doesn't want to be killed?"

"Then we won't find it."

"Have you ever found one and let it go?"

"That's ridiculous," he says. He throws his arm. The whip snaps in the air. The force of the sound splits against the skin of his face. The dogs mush forward.

***

Normally Kesuk does the hunt with Akhlut, the mayor, along with a pair of young adults that changes year by year. High school graduates that weren't going to college, typically. They'd be trained for two months prior to the hunt. This year, there were no young volunteers and the two months were spent training this crew.

Kesuk had at least wanted Akhlut around. Before they left, Kesuk asked a last time, "Are you sure you don't want to lead?"

This trip is the first time where Kesuk is not only the most experienced hunter, but the only one with any experience at all. It worries him. What if he can't find the bear? When the new hunters are Inuit, he gets worried enough as it is, fearing that he might slip up, might identify a break in the snow as an animal when it is really the result of a strong gust, might lead the team over a too-thin layer of ice and doom them all. Now he has to represent his entire culture, their entire way of life, to be absorbed into this camera eye.

Akhlut had laughed at his worry. "You will do fine. And you're ready for this. I'm getting too old to keep hunting, you know."

"I have luck working against me."

"The spirits don't care what their skin color is, Kesuk."

He tried again, desperately this time. "I'm not ready for this, Akhlut. How should I know what the spirits want?"

The mayor patted Kesuk on the back. "The only rule to follow is to pay attention to the world. When you do that, you will see the truth of things. I believe in you."

Now Kesuk ponders Yolanda's question. Had Akhlut ever found a bear and let her go? If so, Kesuk doesn't think he would have even noticed. He wonders sometimes all the things he fails to notice amidst this vast whiteness and the seemingly magical way that Akhlut could find tracks or spot fecal droppings in the snow from three kilometers away.

From the monitor stuffed into his ear canal, there is a crunch of static, followed by Mark's voice. "Hey, Chad and I both saw some dark spots in the snow back there."

Kesuk says, "What?"

"There are these little spots along the trail now."

Kesuk studies the snow ahead of his dogs. Immediately, he groans and curses. "Good eye," he says. Of course he'd seen these intermittent splotches in the snow, but he didn't think about it. Most of the year, Kesuk hunts smaller game on proper land, and disturbed snow is often dotted with debris, dirt, mud and clay kicked up from beneath. But they are on ice right now, not earth. "Those dark spots are blood from a small kill," he explains. "They'll get brighter and redder as we get closer."

"How close are we now?" asks Chad.

"Close."

***

The bear is found not long after. It starts as a small speck, an off-white smudge on the horizon, almost yellow. The dogs begin to bark wildly. They dash. Their yaps are joyful. They run in a prance. Kesuk can now make out the beast. She is staring at him and the dogs. She looks thin. Her belly fat hangs like a curtain from her sides. Her head droops again to the ground. Her nose stirs into a puddle of brown in the snow. The fur on her face is stained berry-red when she looks up again. A seal's blood.

Kesuk reaches down and flips the latch to free the dogs. They run ahead. The sled slides to a stop. He pulls free his rifle. He takes aim. Dogs bark behind him, and then whip past him in a blur of gray. Mark is smarter than Kesuk predicted; he knew to unlatch the dogs from his sled before Kesuk could even give the order.

Kesuk asks, "Look behind. Mark hopped onto Chad's sled, right?"

"Yeah, I see them."

"Good," he says, lining his sights and waiting for the dogs.

The bear roars. She stands on her haunches. Eight feet tall, maybe. She slaps at the dogs whirring around her, but they are fast and trained to dodge and distract her. The battle lifts lumps of snow into the air that burst into crystal dust. The floating frost fractures the sunlight; a halo is cast around the beast.

Mark and Chad slide up beside Kesuk. Mark is laughing. "Hoo boy! Glad as shit we put cameras on their collars!"

Kesuk barks, "Shut up. And watch. She lets herself be taken, see? She stands and reveals her heart to us." He fires. The beast yelps and drops onto her front paws again.

He looks at Mark with a grin. Mark frowns. "I was hoping for something more climatic."

The dogs are still barking. When Kesuk looks again at the bear, he sees a splotch of blood on her arm. She is staring at him. A roar rips through her throat. She charges, bowling through the dogs encircling her. Kesuk yanks on his rifle's bolt. The breech spits out a cartridge. He fishes in his pocket for another round.

Chad croaks, "Oh shit!"

In his periphery, Kesuk can see the two men turning. He cries, "Don't!" But they are already running. The bear is already giving chase. "You *stupid* children!" Kesuk's heart stampedes beneath his breastbone. He jams the round into his rifle's breech. The bear bellows another roar, closing in on the men. She swipes an arm and strikes both to the ground. She stands above them and raises her arm again.

Next, a deafening boom. A spray of blood. The beast falling

to her side. And Kesuk's brief fit of laughter.

The beast growls gently with each breath. Kesuk keeps his gun raised. The dogs try to rush the scene; Kesuk yelps the halt command. They stop at once; some sit and others whine and beg and plead. Mark belts from the ground, "I think my arm's broken!"

Kesuk barks back, "Shut up! She's still alive." He quickly assesses the fallen bundle of fur. The second shot hit the same arm as the first.

Yolanda asks from behind, "Please tell me everyone has their microphones on." There is a chorus of *nopes*. She sighs heavily. "And why aren't we killing the bear?"

Kesuk responds, "It's downed. Not very gentlemanly, is it?"

"You were laughing when you shot it!"

He chuckles. "I didn't expect the white men to get mauled. I mean, that's pretty funny, isn't it?"

Mark groans. "Still here. Still hurt."

Now Chad speaks from the ground above Mark's head. "Can I get up? I just have some scratches from falling."

Kesuk commands, "No one move. She's rising."

The bear rolls over. She staggers her way to a stand. Her right arm is dotted twice in red. It collapses beneath her weight and she plops down again with a grunt. A plume of snow lifts around her and crashes over Mark like an ocean wave. He begins to whimper. The bear makes another climb to her feet. This time, she pulls her shoulders back and up. She pivots at her hips until she is up again on her haunches. She turns and looks at Kesuk, her arms hanging by her side. Again, she reveals herself, opens herself to the shot.

Kesuk looks up into the bear's eyes. His rifle is steady, pointed at her heart once again. He looks at her wounded arm briefly. Both shots look clean, far from bone. The bullets probably tore straight through her. She can heal from this.

She straightens even more and Kesuk realizes she has been hunching over. She stretches taller. Her head and shoulders block out the afternoon sun. Kesuk is bathed in her shadow. Her left arm rises; she covers both wounds with a single paw. It covers his shot, but he can shoot her head or her neck easily.

He lowers the rifle. She shifts her weight onto one leg and takes three clumsy side-steps to turn around. She begins to waddle

away. The dogs try to move again after her. Kesuk reminds them
to stay. Next, he drops his rifle in the ice and walks to Mark and
Chad. "You can get up," he says to Chad. And then he looks at
Mark. "You, don't move." He kneels and produces a knife as Chad
climbs to his feet and immediately fixes his camera onto the scene.

Kesuk slips the blade into Mark's coat sleeve at the wrist
and cuts up along the length of it. The sleeve splits open like a blanket unrolling. White and gray feathers spill onto the snow; some
are dyed red from blood. Kesuk begins to poke at Mark's wounds.
"It isn't so bad," he says. He cleans away the blood and fraying flesh
of Mark's upper arm. The humerus was snapped during the first
mauling; a splintered point of bone spears through the skin. "How
do you feel?"

Mark doesn't move. His eyes fix on Kesuk for a moment
and then roll away. He mutters, "Cold. And this hurts pretty good."

Kesuk nods slowly. "We'll need to splint that arm up," he
says, walking over to his sled and pulls a hatchet from it, then
moves to the seal carcass the bear had been feeding on. He grips
one of the seal's fins, hacks at the joint until it's been freed, and then
quickly carves flesh and fur from bone. Kesuk thrusts his knife into
the elbow joint and forcefully pries the humerus from the rest of
the arm, sawing the sinew as it stretches thin. His gloves are now
soaked in ice water and blood. His fingers stiffen; movement becomes laborious.

He returns to Mark, carrying the seal's bone in his hand,
which leaves a line of run blood steaming in the snow. He kneels
and grips Mark's forearm near the elbow. He grits his teeth. He
yanks hard. The protruding bone near Mark's shoulder recedes
with a snap and a slurp.

Mark yowls in pain.

Small pools of water appear by his eyes. He tries to roll over
toward the injured arm and Kesuk punches the man's left shoulder
down, stapling him to the snow. Mark then shuts his eyes tight.
He shouts, "God! Fuck! Jesus fuck! Even the tears hurt!" His wails
degrade to laughter. "Fuck," he says again.

Kesuk ignores him. As he bandages the arm and splint with
the torn sleeve fabric, he keeps stealing glances at the bear walking
away from them, shrinking into the distance. Chad's camera moves
around Kesuk's head like an orbiting moon. Chad says, "You let it

go."

He nods. "I let it go."

"Why?" asked Yolanda.

Kesuk grunts as he finishes tying the splint. He answers, "She moved her arm over her chest three times. I was wrong. Clearly, she doesn't want to be downed today." He scoops his arm beneath Mark's back and hoists him to his feet. "How do you feel?"

"Awful."

Kesuk nods. He looks at the others and then at the sleds. He says to the others, "Let's re-harness the dogs and get out of here." They call the dogs back to the sleds and harness them in again. Kesuk keeps looking up at the bear in the distance; he notes her awkward gait as she shuffles through the snow, how she can melt into the vast whiteness and reappear step by step, how she sometimes falls and stands again. He notices that Chad is no longer filming them; he too has his camera fixed on the bipedal bear inching toward the horizon. There is a moment when she turns her head and looks behind her, back at them and the barking dogs. Kesuk can't tell if she is looking directly at him or at the camera's eye—it is too far to discern, but he's certain that it's one of the two. She turns back around and continues her walking. A gust of wind kicks up the snow around her. She doesn't pause or shield herself or turn her back to the wind. She continues to promenade through the frosted fog. Kesuk doesn't look away until the whole of her figure has been obscured by the curtain of rising snow.

Once I Wed a White Woman

"I've never dated an Asian before," she said when we sat down, covering a breathy laugh with only three fingers. A small stretch of smile remained exposed, creeping out from behind her hand. It was our first date. I took her to my favorite sushi bar. There were three Korean men behind the bar slicing sashimi and using bamboo mats to roll rice and seaweed in the Japanese fashion. At first, I called her the girl to all my friends. The girl was tall and blonde, had that towering sort of stature that made many men uncomfortable. I probably would have been too, if I weren't so used to being the smaller one in relationships. She asked, "So what are you again?"

I shrugged. Her eyes kept flicking away from mine to the glass wall by the entrance. I turned around once to see what was distracting her. Just pedestrians. White folk ambling to their dinners or movies or CrossFit classes after work. Little more than illusions of form and color gliding across the glass, catching her attention the way a moving dust mote does a cat. I replied, "You first."

She straightened. Her lips pulled toward one side of her face. An eyebrow curved upward. I smiled. She hooked a wisp of her yellow hair behind an ear and chuckled. Her eyes darted down for just a moment. "Oh, a joke, huh? I get it."

"My parents are Vietnamese." I kept my smile up.

Later, we went two blocks down to a bar with blacklights and hip hop music. The walls wore abstract murals of fluorescent paint, all angles and diagonals that seemed, under the violet lamps, to leap angrily out to the center of the room. We stood at the bar.

She drank vodka tonic with a lime wedge. I drank bourbon with three ice cubes. She was tall enough that I had to look up to her. She asked, "Do you dance?"

I answered, "I have no sense of rhythm."

"Don't you play an instrument? Piano?"

I couldn't remember if I had told her that or not. I laughed and nodded. "Yeah. Not piano though. Just guitar."

"Oh really? What kind of music do you play? I love acoustic guitar. It's one of the most beautiful instruments, don't you think?"

I nodded again. I said, "I play in a local death metal band."

"A what band?" She showed me her ear. My eyes fell to her cleavage for a moment when she looked away. I dragged my attention up her chest, over the crest of her collarbone, along the slope of her neck, and then to her small ear. It wasn't pierced. I liked that. I had an urge then to bite the lobe, to tongue along the canal.

"Death metal," I said louder.

When she faced me again, she squinted at first. And then she made quarters of her eyes. She said, "Oh." She bit her lower lip. She sipped her vodka tonic.

"And jazz," I added.

Now she beamed. She touched my arm, exclaiming excitedly, "Really? Who do you like? Holiday? Or do you prefer more classic stuff? Fitzgerald and Armstrong?" Her fingers were cold, moistened from the cold glass of her drink. It was crowded and though we stood close, she leaned in closer still, like she couldn't risk my response getting lost in the noise surrounding us. Where her body didn't press against my skin, her heat did. I could see now that my eyes came to her nose. When she exhaled, her breath carried the taste of her lips to my own.

I didn't have a good answer for her. She'd only named singers and I believed real jazz had no room for singers. Words were obstructions; music was to be heard, not listened to.

I took her wrist and pulled her onto the dance floor. She moved well with the music, her hips popping or pivoting at each beat. I could always time my wrist to a drum, but never my hips. Different kinds of rhythm. Different kinds of movement. I moved like a crab next to her, awkward and off-time. She laughed at me. She called me cute when I blushed.

Later, I took her home. We walked up the stairs to her

fourth floor apartment. Her door was painted the color of creamed coffee. She turned the knob and then her body twisted to face me again, her shoulder blades pressing against the door, opening it with her weight. She clasped her hands around my wrists and pulled me in with her. She didn't expect how easily I would be led by her, and so we fell against a wall. A large down coat dropped from its hook over her right shoulder. It curtained her head and shoulders. I swam through the fabric to find her face again, led by her giggling. We kissed. She tasted faintly of lime. She smelled of mint. She kicked the door closed.

***

When I first moved into my apartment, I framed a poem that the Buddha recites at the end of *The Diamond Sutra* and hung it up on the wall over my bed. I chose birch for the frame. The grain was mostly an amber color, striped with black.

There is a copy of the sutra that is considered the oldest printed book known to history, pre-dating the Gutenberg Bible by nearly six hundred years. The text appears on silk scrolls using thick sheets of engraved birch bark to press the script. In it, the Buddha encourages his disciple Subhuti not to cling to concepts, but to accept the nature of reality as change itself. Suffering is the delusion that things can remain as they are.

The poem reads:

> *All composed things are like a dream,*
> *a phantom, a drop of dew, a flash of lightning.*
> *That is how to meditate on them,*
> *That is how to observe them.*

***

Three months later, the girl had become the girlfriend. It was May. She met my family at a Mother's Day dinner. "Isn't it weird to always do family dinners at a Chinese buffet?" she asked in the car.

I shrugged. "My dad won't eat white food."

"There's a white food?"

"American food," I corrected myself.

"Does he eat anything that isn't Asian?" she asked.

I had just pulled into a parking spot in the strip mall. I was staring at the bright red letters above the door that read "PETER PAN BUFFET." I asked, "Does Indian food count?"

"No. That's still Asian."

"Yeah, well, I mean, technically." She laughed at me and slapped my arm. "Okay, no, he doesn't. I mean, he will, but he doesn't like to."

Stepping inside the restaurant, everything became red and gold. There was a hint of ginseng in each breath. The clatter of carving knives came spitting toward us from the far end of the room. The cooks were sharpening their tools; they were slicing roasts from behind a glass sneeze-guard and a curtain of hissing steam. My family sat at a large circular table for six: my parents, my brother and his also-white girlfriend were already seated. Their plates were empty.

"Sorry we're late," I said.

No one spoke. My brother shrugged, his lips a left-leaning line. I pulled a seat back for the girlfriend. She sat. The others stood and departed the table. The girlfriend looked at me, her mouth open, astonished. I answered, "They're getting food." She still looked confused. I explained, "We don't really talk to each other. Not much."

I started for the plates. When the girlfriend appeared behind me, I handed her one. She said, "You just walked away from me."

I raised an eyebrow. "Did you want us to sit until they came back to fill our plates?"

"No, I mean, you didn't say anything."

"I don't get it."

She sighed and shook her head and then walked around me to the row of stainless steel trays and shoveled a mound of fried noodles onto her plate. I thought she was upset, but when she picked up a prawn that had been cooked straight, she pointed it out to me with a smile. It lay limp on her dish beside the wet brown tangle of noodles. "Kinda creepy, huh?" She placed a curled prawn beside it.

I nodded. I said, "The straight one seems more dead."

Everyone was already seated and eating when we returned to the table. My mother asked, "So how is everything?"

And I answered, "Okay, I think."

We talked briefly about nothing. My brother and I then engaged in a conversation about recent video games. I paid the bill. The girlfriend and I stood and waved our goodbyes. She asked quietly, "Why did you pay the bill for the whole family?"

I whispered, "I'm the eldest son. That's how it works."

When we were back in the car, the girlfriend stared at me. I asked, "What?" I turned the ignition. The engine coughed into a start.

She asked, "You don't hug your mother goodbye?" Her eyes looked wet.

I answered, "I don't hug my mother at all."

***

It is said in Buddhism that all phenomena arise from causes and conditions. This is the doctrine of interdependent origination. It is said that because the concept of "self" can only be defined through its relationships to other objects or persons—a person can be defined as a mother or son, friend or foe, bourgeois or proletariat, woman or man, etc.—that the self therefore can only exist as a construction of convenience. It is a delusion. We only exist through our relationships. We are nothing more than a web of interlocking phenomena enduring the same causal process of change. Loneliness is just a consequence of ego; it is the delusion of independence.

***

A year passed. The girlfriend moved into my apartment. We had been living together for a single spring, and were a month into the summer. We took down my altar to Gautama Buddha and moved it into a corner of the bedroom. We put up framed pictures of ourselves. We took down the ribbons of red silk scarves, which wore swastikas stitched in gold thread, from my walls; we replaced them with works of art that meant nothing but looked pretty. I had known for years that I had to eventually take them down, but it still bothered me. Westerners couldn't look at a swastika without a sense of shame, and so I was supposed to feel this shame too. Shame for my own faith.

Now I came home to my culture in a corner. And change kept coming. The next month, the girlfriend said she wanted a new bed. "That's ridiculous. We have a king," I said.

"You have a platform bed," she said.

"So?"

"It's too low to the ground."

"I like low to the ground."

"I don't," she said. "It makes me feel uncomfortable. Like someone could come in and walk all over me."

"Okay, okay, maybe I get it. It's a white thing, right? The high chairs thing. The high bed thing." I tried to flash a smile. I shrugged my shoulders with a peaceful smirk. "And this is an Asian thing, right? I'm short and all. Like an oompa-loompa."

She appeared in the doorway, grinning. "Not everything's about race, asshole. I just like feeling like I'm floating on my mattress. Sleeping near the ground is a little depressing, isn't it?"

I paused. I told her, "You have a good point." She had strange ways of showing her affection, but she was often right. There was something dark about descending into your own sheets, each night literally putting yourself down. I admitted, "Maybe it could help my mood." She nodded slowly, and then crossed over to me. She threaded her arms beneath mine, embraced me softly. I kissed her left temple. I thanked her for releasing me from my own dogmas, but I didn't know if I believed myself.

***

One of the Buddha's titles is also a description of reality itself: *Tathagata*, thus come, thus gone. When we meditate on the nature of this name, we are told to contemplate that all objects we hold in our minds have already gone, that we hold onto empty vessels, deluding ourselves into believing in their substance and their permanence.

Twenty-eight Tathagatas arose, abided, and passed into extinction. Neither the Buddhas nor their dharma can endure. All that arises ceases.

Every moment is always an ending.

***

The fiancée loved to travel. She said she wanted to experience other cultures, to gain worldly perspective. She had to leave home to understand and so did I, even if she needed an airport and I needed a driveway. We went to Thailand. We had different concepts of culture. She wanted to bike from city to city and I wanted to visit monasteries. She wanted to experience how the Thai enjoyed dance clubs and I wanted to meet the Thai Forest monks who had achieved arhantship—nirvana, the cessation of birth. She said, "I don't believe in enlightenment." I wondered how anyone could go through life without believing—or at least hoping—for a reprieve from consciousness. But then I remembered that only atheists, Buddhists and Confucians believe in liberation and I felt a pang of empathy for the rest of the world, for everyone who wanted to keep living, to endure suffering for eternity.

The fiancée and I chose instead to compromise: we visited an animal sanctuary. The entrance was a short bamboo fence that rose to the middle of my belly. I couldn't believe how the elephants behind it were contained. They could have smashed down the wall with flicks of their trunks if they wanted to. I wondered if they knew they were caged. I wondered if they cared. The fences would break down eventually anyway.

We sat on a young elephant named Khunying. She was peacefully pulling chunks of a split melon into her mouth with her trunk. In the distance, beyond another fence, was a platoon of adult elephants standing in a circle, all facing each other. We watched; minutes passed. Every so often, we could see their trunks stretching skyward and then falling again. Occasionally, one or two elephants would retreat from the circle and walk around, picking up sticks and branches. They'd drop their sticks on the ground over other sticks and then pick up the whole bundle, wrapping it up in their trunks. When their bundles became sizeable, they returned to the circle, squeezed themselves between two behemoth bodies. The clatter of falling sticks came to us as a cascade of quiet clicks. The fiancée said, "I wonder what they're doing."

"Sort of looks like they're building a campfire," I said.

"Funeral," said Khunying's handler who stood to our right. He had a palm on the elephant's side and beside my leg in case she decided she wanted to throw us off or something. He was a thin man, brown-skinned, and was dressed in a blue jumpsuit. He gave us a snaggle-toothed smile. "Bury friend."

"Funeral," I repeated with a nod. I looked back at the creatures. I squinted. I could see between their legs; I could see the mound of mud and branches and leaves at their center, a coffin of the earth itself.

***

We call the cycle of births samsara. The Tathagata described all things as cycles. The universe repeats cycles of expansion and collapse. Not even the dharma endures. It too dies and is reborn as something different.

The girlfriend has been reborn six times. She is always someone new. Once, the girlfriend was unfaithful. Once, the girlfriend was cheated on. Once, the girlfriend was born as the fiancée. Once, the girlfriend became the wife, and she passed into extinction.

***

Four months after Thailand, we were married in her hometown where her parents had wed. She'd wanted a traditional ceremony in a church. I mentioned early on, "Neither of us are Christian."

She said, "I just want a normal wedding."

The church was a small building with white walls. From the gutters at the edge of the roof hung ribbons of rust that settled into the paint, staining it in oranges and browns and ambers. The paint had cracked and formed fissures at the corners of all the door and window frames. I thought about the space between the cracks, how a house of God wore rivers of absence.

The pews inside were glossed in a chocolate finish. There were kaleidoscopes for windowpanes that cast color over our clothes and our skin. A man in a black robe talked to us about togetherness and God and eternity. I stopped listening.

In her vow, she promised to love me unconditionally.
In mine, I didn't.

***

I heard a monk once say that Buddhists could not honestly
believe in marriage. "Love cannot last forever," he said. "Nothing
can."

I was a college student then. I was a young man. I was angry at him. I asked, "So why do we marry?"

He said, "Don't misunderstand. Love is a gift we are not
meant to keep."

He said, "Marriage is the delusion we can keep love forever."

He said, "No one can promise forever. People change into
other people. You were a boy. Now you are a man. Next you will
be an old man. You are never the same person. You can be a man
one moment and a woman another. You cannot promise to love
someone forever. You can only promise to cherish love as it lasts."

He said, "Divorce. Now, divorce, Buddhists can get behind." He laughed and when he laughed his face folded at the
cheeks and braced the sides of his up-curved mouth, like his lips
were a parenthetical note for his argument.

***

Once, when she was the wife, I convinced her to go on a
meditation retreat with me. We drove for seven hours. The road
went from asphalt to gravel and back again. Then the road became
dirt and the buildings around us became trees and the emptiness
before us became a monastery that was a small cabin.

Inside, we knelt on pillows in a large room, painted red like
berries, where the walls wore golden ornaments—octagon charms
called mandalas, or else swastikas. We listened to monks in brown
robes chant in a foreign language. Before us was a Buddha, legs
braided together beneath his robes. He sat on a throne that was
a bowl formed from giant lotus petals. He was the color of light
itself; an empty smile pulled up the ends of his lips. His eyes were
frozen open. From the ground, thin ribbons of smoke stretched

up and faded below his golden gleaming chin. When the chanting ceased, silence came. The kneeling worshippers all fell forward; we pressed our foreheads to the ground. The carpet smelled of ginseng. Spilled tea, I thought.

We sat in the stillness for an hour. When the wife started snoring, I nudged her awake.

Later, we walked in the woods. Chirping birds peppered the air. The wife and I diverged from the group and found a place where a razor blade of sunlight sliced through the tree branches. We sat facing each other. She was sluggish getting to the ground. She looked partway in a dream. There was darkness under her eyes and crow's feet crackling out from the corners. "This is the most boring thing in the world," she said. "I don't get it."

"You just have to focus," I told her. "Focus on this moment. Right now. Don't let your mind carry you away from here. Don't think about home. Don't think about work. Or the future. Or the past." I reached out. I took her hands. I pulled them into my lap. "Focus on this moment," I said again.

"I can't," she said. "I try and it just isn't there. There isn't anything to focus on." Her eyes welled with water; sunlight broke against the surface of her tears.

"Exactly," I said. She looked at me. "It isn't there," I repeated. When she pulled her hands from my lap, I thought for a moment that she understood. But she didn't speak again. She was there in the moment—the moment I spoke of—and she kept on looking at me as if there was something there to see, as if I weren't already gone.

The Golden Turtle God

Mr. Le joined the maintenance crew for Hoan Kiem Lake as a volunteer not long after returning to Viet Nam. The lake had become noxious in its pollution and the government of Hanoi feared the turtle could survive for only a short time more. He threw on a jumpsuit every day, waded the shallow perimeters collecting garbage. When the coordinator discovered he had been a chemist before the war, Mr. Le was also charged with rowing to the center of the lake to collect samples. They wanted to analyze pH levels, PCB content, and nitrogen saturation—any data that could have proved useful in saving the hallowed lake. From time to time, Mr. Le saw the white and silver lips of fish break the surface of the water, sucking up miniscule debris for food, before submerging again into the depths. When this happened, he leaned over the edge of his canoe, stretched his neck to get a glimpse of what creature might have surfaced. There was a chance that it could be the great turtle, that he would receive the divine blessing of the gods.

The god-beast first appeared in the fifteenth century when it gifted the hero Le Loi with a heavenly sword. The sword was used to unite Viet Nam and drive back the Chinese. Out of respect to the gods, Le Loi returned the sword to Hoan Kiem Lake and the golden turtle god grasped it in his beak to deliver it back to the heavens. The turtle was given the name Cu Rua, the "Great Grandfather" of Viet Nam.

Last year, a net tangled itself with the golden turtle. It had been nearly a century since the Cu Rua's last appearance. The lake was swarmed; even the southerners went on pilgrimage at a chance to see the divine turtle. They left offerings of rice at the lake's edge and burnt incense in the turtle's honor. While biologists—who had discovered the turtle was sick—worked to restore the creature's health, Mr. Le was still in America watching the slow decline of his wife.

When Mr. Le heard of Cu Rua's return, he searched for and read everything he could on it. How the turtle was trapped. How the turtle was sickly, lesions splotched all over its body. How, contrary to the stories, Cu Rua was female. And Mr. Le thought, How fantastic! Mr. Le was staying outside of Hanoi with distant relatives when he began taking day trips to Hoan Kiem Lake, a venerated location within the city walls. He rode a Honda 1961 moped, more rust than engine, out to the lake and detoured to his old friend Hoang's temple for dinner and tea before bed. It felt appropriate: his days at the hallowed lake, his evenings in the temple, his nights alone. Mr. Le thought that if he could connect again to the heavens, he would not feel so alone. He could be reassured. He could touch some remaining fragment of Mrs. Le.

***

Mrs. Le had fallen to a cancer that took her legs two years ago. Those days, Mr. Le could be found at her hospital bed, clutching her bony limp hand in his grip. Her skin sagged into neat columns of wrinkles and her cheeks were sucked in. Mr. Le looked his wife in the eyes, promised her it would be okay, that the chemo would exorcise the cancer.

She was his wife for fifty-two years. It was hard for him to look at her eyes and see how they had aged so suddenly, recessed in her skull. The moment the cancer finally took Mrs. Le, her eyes were closed and relief stirred something rancid in his stomach.

He flew with Mrs. Le back to Viet Nam for the funeral. A rusted saw buzzed inside him on the plane and then thrashed wildly during the wake. His old friends came, tied white strips of cloth across their foreheads in respect. Afterward, they drank with him. They helped to bury the pain in rice wine. Mr. Le couldn't remember these people. He had spent so long away their faces had been scrubbed smooth in his memory. Their friendship felt mechanical. A performance of duty and ritual. Any fraternity had been burned in napalm forty years ago. An old monk bowed his head to Mr. Le and said the prayer, "*Adida Phat,* Professor." The monk's voice was soaked with a very personal compassion. It directed itself into Mr. Le, made a home of his heart and warmed him. He thought maybe the holy voice could eat away the fermenting poison. When he looked up, his mind smoothed out the wrinkles of the monk's face and saw that it was Hoang.

"When did you become a monk?" he asked through an unexpected smile.

"A lot can change in forty years," answered Hoang.

Mr. Le's eyes fell away as he nodded his agreement. This was not the Viet Nam he remembered. It was no longer rolling hills, pink lotus flowers, and the calming wash of a waterfall, the way it was still depicted in watercolor paintings he found in America. Hanoi returned to him a city whose veins were populated with millions of cone-hats and bodies on bicycles. His lungs filled with the stench of their sweat, the musk that came with old age and poverty and the molded rot that came from some homeless man's putrid shit in an alleyway. His rolling hills were only the black mounds of the cyclists' heads. His waterfall was only the drench of collective sweat that slicked the streets.

Hoang—bald, robed, smiling serenely as if the world hadn't been eviscerated—was a relic, an echo of another world. "I am sorry for your loss. She was a wonderful woman. If you need to talk, you should visit the temple." The monk placed his hand on Mr. Le's shoulder. It halted the quiet desperation for a moment, the tiny ruptures in his soul that divided day by day, like new-born baby cells in mitosis. When Hoang removed his hand, there was a vacuum.

***

Weeks passed. Mr. Le went to the lake every day and the temple every night. Rueful words spilled into the temple, entwining with the curling threads of smoke that lifted from incense sticks. Hoang offered Buddhist teachings like fortune cookie wisdoms. *Let your grief be only a moment in the river of consciousness. Or, Death is in the nature of life.* Suffering stems from the delusion that life will not change. The words did little to help. They stirred

Mr. Le's anger.

Mr. Le studied Hoang's face each night, noting the peaceful way his skin and musculature surrendered into the bones of his skull. When Mr. Le looked at himself in the mirror, he saw knots of tension pulling his brow down and his lips back. Hoang's face revealed nothing of the war, not the way that Mr. Le saw sculpted into his own. He wanted to claim that sense of peace for himself, to wholly devour Hoang's enlightenment.

One night, Mr. Le admitted that he volunteered on the lake in hopes of seeing Cu Rua. Hoang said, "The turtle hides for centuries sometimes. I don't understand your persistence. Whole generations go by without seeing the turtle."

"Did you see the turtle last year?"

"When the biologists came to heal it? No, I did not. It is an old tale, my friend. One of superstition and mythology." Hoang smoothed out the waves of folding fabric from his robes. When Mr. Le scowled, he added, "Of course the turtle is real. We have photographs. But it is just a turtle."

"The turtle is a god," said Mr. Le. "It is written into our history books!"

"A god that only appears when she is sick and dying?" Hoang shook his head slowly. "I am not one to believe in gods."

"You're supposed to be a holy man."

"The people of Viet Nam are too fixed in the ancient myths. Buddhism does not care for theism."

"But you used to."

"Yes, I did. But I used to believe in a lot of things."

Hoang had supported the Viet Minh in driving out the French; he had been an idealist revolutionary. When Mr. Le made the decision to leave for America, his colleagues accused him of siding with the democratic separatists in the south. They were wrong. Nowhere was there a greater disdain for the illusion of democracy than Mr. Le. He was not a Communist for the mere reason that he was a pessimist. He shared none of Hoang's optimism, none of the fire to fight for a better world. And Mr. Le loved his wife more than he loved his country. He wanted to be with her somewhere that they never again would hear the tin squeal of a descending bomb as its pitch plummeted in octaves, wondering if death was waiting for the song to scale to its lowest note.

Mr. Le could see Hoang no longer believed in the regime. He wondered how his friend could be so at peace when he had lost both his countries and his gods. The mystery invaded him as he tried to sleep that night. Maybe Cu Rua would unravel that puzzle as well. Maybe the turtle could reveal to Mr. Le how the monk could at once be so faithless and so exalted.

***

His thoughts were collisions of grief and blasphemy as he collected his samples. The turtle had been sick when it was found. Maybe it had died. Maybe this was an era where gods could die. One morning, he rowed far into the center of the lake and positioned himself so that Thap Rua, the monument called Turtle Tower, drew a line between the lake and the sky in his vision. When he leaned over the side of the canoe, thrust his hands deep into the green murk of the lake to uproot seaweed, he meditated on how the tower's reflection warped. The water's oscillation tore the tower into pixels and rearranged all its parts; then it tethered the tower back together before shredding it up again. Mr. Le thought maybe the gods were born and died and reborn like the buddhas.

The previous night Hoang had asked, "Why are you still here?" Mr. Le was taken aback. He thought his friend was asking him to leave. Then he clarified, "In Viet Nam. You live in America now. Why stay here for so long?"

"I won't leave until I see Cu Rua," answered Mr. Le. "The gods owe me their blessing."

Hoang sighed heavily, rose and left Mr. Le on the temple floor. His robes disappeared through a door. After twenty minutes, Mr. Le turned to the gold statue of Amida Buddha seated upon a giant lotus, painted black, the petals of which formed a bowl for the Buddha. He wore an empty smile curled on his lips. His eyes were frozen open. From the floor, incense sticks stretched for the Buddha's face in thin ribbons of smoke that faded just below the Great One's golden gleaming chin. Mr. Le bowed his head to the floor. It smelled of ginseng. He unfolded at the hips and then offered two more prostrations. He clasped his hands together at his forehead and chanted in Vietnamese an excerpt of the *Amitabha Sutra*. When his chanting ceased, silence came like a guillotine.

***

Hoang was not at the temple for the next two days when Mr. Le came after finishing his work at the lake. He sat with other monks each evening for a short time before retiring back to the room his relatives had allowed him in their home outside Hanoi. He lay in the small hard bed, in darkness, reflecting on what his old friend—or what any monk, for that matter—might be doing away from the temple. From the floorboards came the raucous of Mr. Le's relatives playing card games over night time tea, roars and laughter and applause. Perhaps Hoang was visiting family. His grandchildren, perhaps.

Yes, of course! Family.

Hoang's son, Khoa, had opened a bookstore during the war with France. It had been in the old gambling district where men, in the 40s, secretly retreated late at night, after their wives had fallen asleep, to gamble on card games and cock fights. Hoang had been a regular, although Mr. Le hadn't known why until after the revolution broke out. There had been whispers the intellectuals traded coded essays through the card decks, whole discourses on rights and injustices. The coup had started on playing cards.

When morning came, Mr. Le opened a book of maps and tried to recall from memory where the bookstore had been. He scrawled the address onto a scrap of paper and folded into his back pocket before leaving to collect seaweed at the lake. When he was done for the day, the sun was still slung high into the sky. He waited on the water for an extra hour, hoping and praying for any sign of the turtle. His thoughts drifted to Mrs. Le, the clouds forming a perfect picture of her. And this caused him to double over and weep. The surface waves formed a carpet of mitts to catch the sound of his cries. He cursed the gods before he left; he was owed this blessing. As Mr. Le rowed angrily back across the vast and godless surface of the lake, his eyes snagged on something in the water. Something moving. Something goliath burst open the skin of the lake.

***

Mr. Le sped his moped to Hoang's address. The gambling

district had dilapidated since Mr. Le left Hanoi. The buildings, squeezed tightly side-by-side, seemed to stand in sad deflated postures. When he knocked on the door of an old building, it shook loosely from its hinges. Mr. Le peered through the crack between the door and its frame. There was a dim light that undulated in its luminescence and told Mr. Le that it was candle light. He heard his old friend's voice. "Come in."

So Hoang was here.

It was a small room. Rows of dusty shelves were bolted to the walls on all sides, save for a small doorway in the far corner. There was an outline on the wooden floor where a counter had once been. On one of the shelves was a small glass oil lamp, a tiny tongue of flame licking the air. Mr. Le assumed this was a bookstore or a video rental before it had been abandoned. Hoang sat lotus on the ground in the center. He smiled.

"Did Khoa lose the store?" asked Mr. Le.

Hoang slowly brought himself up to his feet. "Did I ever tell you why I became a monk?" Mr. Le didn't answer; the two hadn't seen each other in forty years since the funeral. They never talked or exchanged letters. Hoang took the oil lamp from its shelf and began walking toward the back door. Mr. Le followed. "After you left and the Americans came, the Viet Cong marched through Hanoi to recruit. They spoke of patriotism."

They walked down a staircase. Mr. Le wanted to tell Hoang about the afternoon and ask his opinion on what had occurred, but it was a rude thing to interrupt. He remained silent.

"While the intellectuals brought Communism, they could not maintain power. You see, education is privilege and we were fighting for the peasant class. Suddenly the whole world changed; our culture became fixated on suppressing the intellectuals. Real men, productive men, work the rice paddies. They do not read books."

The room at the bottom of the steps was barren save for a wooden table whose surface was cut as an octagon. Even in the poor glow of the lamp, Mr. Le could see the thick gray layer of dust like a sheet of wool draped over the wood. "How is your family?" asked Hoang as he set the lamp on the table. He bowed his head down to it, stared at the flame.

Mr. Le's eyes wandered the room. The ceiling was low; spiders had ornamented each corner in polygonal lines of woven silk. He couldn't think to answer the question. Mrs. Le was everything. He responded, "The heavens owe me a blessing."

"The heavens owe nothing." Hoang's face softened with concern. His voice came with weakness, tinged with love. "The heavens cannot heal you."

Mr. Le did not admit that he lost the very world. He would not admit—not to Hoang—that the lake felt like a private plane of existence all for him, that he would live on that boat if he could, rest between the earth and the heavens, the air and the sea, until he could be carried off to death. His private shame was that he fought every day to not leap into the lake and bury himself in water. Worse, he could not articulate why he fought at all. He could not convince himself why rowing back to land was a good idea. He had wanted to dive after the turtle, but the undulating surface of the water had seemed a barrier. The divine below, the wicked earth above.

This was the opportunity to tell Hoang about what happened this afternoon on the lake. Mr. Le opened his mouth, but Hoang's voice came first. "You never asked how my son was," said Hoang. His eyes still were fixed on the flame.

It was true; Mr. Le hadn't even thought to ask. Since Hoang had not mentioned Khoa, Mr. Le assumed the boy had a family elsewhere. The emptied bookstore rewrote this narrative. Now Mr. Le imagined Khoa drafted into the Viet Cong, firing aimlessly into mobs of southern democrats, dying in a fiery blaze where the pops and crackles of sizzling tree sap in the jungle could drown out even the *rat-tat-tat* chorus of rifles.

But Hoang said instead, "He was executed." And now Mr. Le learned how Khoa had fought during the war, not as a soldier but rather for the preservation of Viet Nam's culture. In his idealism, he felt the French had stifled Viet Nam's identity. That the Viet Minh—and later the Viet Cong—were threatening the same. Khoa collected books, reprinted them on a rusted iron press he hid in this basement. Mr. Le saw the stain of oil and ink that colored the concrete ground like a flood of coffee someone lazily mopped away. At ground level, the book store sold only approved titles; beneath were the ancient tales, folklore, the old religions, the Buddhist sutras, the forgotten kung fu manuals from Binh Dinh that had for centuries been banned. All of Viet Nam's rich history contained in four walls, buried under the earth, sharing the same toxic air as the gasoline powering the press. Eventually the regime uncovered Khoa's treason; he was apprehended, jailed for nine months, shot in the forehead one night for an unknown transgression. There was no news of it save for the short three-sentence letter mailed to Hoang by the government.

He laughed softly, the sound from his throat soaked in sadness. It was like the aftermath of a tsunami, all people silent and carrying corpses, the only sound being the slush of water draining from the earth. "Bad luck," said Hoang. "Now religion is legal again—no longer a threat, they said—and the regime is changing. Trying to recover all the lost artifacts of our culture. A matter of national pride, they say! Doing exactly what Khoa was killed for." Hoang placed a hand on Mr. Le's shoulder, like he had done at the funeral. This time, rather than comforting, it seemed a pleading touch. "I became a monk because it was where my grief led me." When he let go and turned away, there was no vacuum. Instead it felt like Hoang had left something behind, had given something dear to Mr. Le. Maybe a hope or a prayer or a gift, he couldn't tell.

Hoang started for the steps and Mr. Le moved to follow. He could feel the shadows converging behind him as Hoang carried the lamp up the stairs. The way the darkness moved back into the room was like an ink well filling up. At the base of the stairs, Mr. Le turned around and stared into the tenebrous space. He marveled at how vast and infinite the room looked without the light. He imagined he could step forward into the blanket of blackness, forward and forward into eternity. Past the far wall of the room. Past the edge of the world. Past the Pure Land of Amitabha Buddha and the entrance of Heaven. On and on to oblivion. He wanted to stay here, in the enormity of the tiny basement, until the darkness could converge on the light of his soul and take him into the infinities. He imagined that here, in this subterranean darkness, was the tunnel to the gods.

It led him back to his memories of the afternoon: a green-yellow bulb like a tree branch enveloped in algae emerging from the water. Its shell broke the surface behind its head like a tiny golden island. It had been as long as he was, as wide as two of him. Cu Rua's shell was the size of Mr. Le's bed. Enormous, beautiful, emerald-gold. He had stretched to touch its head, but Cu Rua slowly backpedaled, drifting from Mr. Le's reach. It blinked once more and then gracefully descended; the scar it opened in the water's surface again closed. Its figure became a dark orb, like the shadow of a new moon, before Mr. Le couldn't see it at all anymore. Then Mr. Le sat back in his canoe, looked up at the heavens. When it was over, everything still ached in a hollow defeated way—his bones, his joints, his stomach and heart. Breathing, thinking, living exhausted him. He hadn't been able to tell if anything at all had changed. He had carried the stillness with him into the basement room. It was only now starting to stir.

Hoang spoke quietly from the top of the steps. His voice slithered down the stairway, bounced and amplified in the acoustics of the small room such that the sound of his words surrounded Mr. Le, who was now drowned in both the monk's divine words and darkness. "I assure you, old friend, what you are looking for is not in that lake."

Mr. Le looked up at Hoang, who was haloed in the light of the doorway. He nodded and climbed the stairs. Outside the bookstore, he thought for a moment to finally tell Hoang what had happened in the lake. But then he remembered how Le Loi returned the heavenly sword to the depths of Hoan Kiem. He thought for the first time that the divine belonged buried below the world and that maybe his blessing had only broken the surface of that water in brevity, had been swallowed in the sutured scar of the lake. Maybe it too belonged there in the dark holy waters.

Extinction with Residue Remaining

One month after their mother passed, Binh called Quan. He said, "I found something." There was no breath punctuating the sentence. Quan didn't respond; it seemed as though his brother had left a thought hanging off that sentence. Dangling in the air. Then Binh added, "It has to do with Ma and Ba. I found it a long time ago. Years ago. In the toys."

"In the toys?"

"In Ba's toys."

"Did you call Tuyet?" asked Quan.

"Yeah, I called her."

"Tonight? After work?"

"Meet at Ma's house."

***

When they were children, their father returned home from work with some toy he found every few months; Ba was a quiet man and never spoke much to his children, but they felt close to him through these gifts. They had no idea where the toys came from, but they were always old and stained and sometimes broken. Once their father brought home a tiny toy piano made of wood. It was the height of a footstool and the top had a deep burgundy stain in the shape of Africa. The keys were the length of half a popsicle stick. There were only two octaves to play in and half the keys were stuck in place. The keys that could be played would lever a hammer into a tiny bell, and a note would *tink* and then be muted. None of the children knew how to play, so they just jammed their hands into the keyboard wildly. The bells chimed in chromatic cacophony; the kids laughed and giggled. For two days, it ate up all of their attention.

On the third day, Tuyet and Quan descended into the basement steps to discover Binh had dismantled the whole thing. He said, "I wanted to find out how it worked." His eyes were cast to the ground. "I can't put it back together again."

"You have to tell Ba," said Tuyet.

"Can't you do it? I don't want him to yell at me."

"When has he ever yelled at anyone? Besides, all the toys he brings home are old and broken anyway." asked Quan.

"Can we do it together?" asked Binh.

"Fine," said Tuyet. "We'll tell him together. But it's still your fault."

When they brought their father into the basement, and he lay his eyes upon the deconstructed piano, he groaned heavily. He turned his head over his shoulder, brought a closed fist to his mouth, and paused there. He turned back around, faced his children, nodded slowly. He knelt and scooped his arms around all three. He said in Vietnamese, "It's okay. It's gone now. There's no getting it back."

It was thrown out that week, a stack of wood sheets and dowels and sticks.

It was always like that. Ba brought home old toys; Binh would take them apart. He almost never managed to put it back together, whatever it was. A toy bird with moving wings and a rotating head was immediately decapitated.

One night, Ba brought home a music box. It was painted in blue with a fine yellow pattern etched into it. A short arm was used to crank and wind the box up, but it didn't work. The only way the box could make music was to very carefully crank the arm backwards, and none of the children could figure out the rhythm to make the song recognizable. Binh took the box into his room. The door shut like a vacuum had sucked it into the frame. Quan and Tuyet knew the next time they saw the box, it wouldn't make any sound at all. But they were used to it, used to Binh's idea of fun being the disassembling of his toys. And so, that night, Tuyet and Quan sat themselves down on the living room couch, trained their eyes to the Discovery Channel nature documentary their father watched from his recliner every night, placing bets on when Binh would be done.

It was days later that Binh reproduced the blue box. When he cranked the arm, the sound of grinding gears buzzed and Tuyet and Quan both stared slack-jawed. Binh grinned, released the arm, and as it began to slowly wind back around, the box sang a metallic version of Fur Elise. When it was done, he scooped the box up in his arms like a cradled baby, ran off to show their father. Quan and his sister watched from the hallway. Binh held up the box in both palms, like he was presenting a gift to a king.

When the tune started, their father smiled at Binh, patted his head, and then his attention eased gently back to the television. When Binh turned to face his siblings again, he was smiling. It was the one and only time Quan could remember Binh smiling with his eyes.

***

When Quan arrived at his parents' house, Binh and Tuyet were already inside, were already arguing again, in the kitchen, over whether or not to sell the house now that Ma was gone. The sound spilled out through a cracked window. Binh already listed it last week, without telling anyone. Quan waited at the door, unsure if he wanted to step inside yet.

Tuyet asked, "Do you really hate Ma and Ba this much? It's our childhood home. Do you have any clue how hard they worked to become landowners in this country?"

Binh said in a quiet monotonous voice, "It's not hatred."

"Our childhood wasn't that bad," argued Tuyet. "Not enough for all this rage you have pent up." Her voice quieted too.

Binh shifted his weight, turning around so he wouldn't have to look at her. He said, "You shouldn't be defending them."

"If they were such awful parents, why did you visit Ma in the hospital so much? I don't get it, Binh. You were there more than we were."

No one had expected that. Every time Quan and Tuyet went to Ma's room together, they'd find Binh there already.

"What do you want me to say?" he asked.

"I want you to admit that you love them and you were hurting and that's why you were there every day and that's why you never said a god damn word to any of us during it."

It didn't matter what they asked or said. Binh didn't speak or cry or even move during those visits. He sat in a chair, elbows propped on his knees, chin resting atop the knuckles of his fisted hands. He stared downward. Not at Ma, but at the ground. Or maybe her bed. He just sat there and stared and said nothing.

"Not any different from how they treated us our whole lives," he retorted.

"So what? It was payback?"

"I was waiting."

"For what? An apology? What the hell did they do!" Tuyet was being loud again.

"Nothing!" he barked. His voice made Quan—still eavesdropping outside—jump up in shock. Now Binh spoke quietly again. "Nothing. They didn't love us or get to know us. They didn't talk to us or tell us anything about themselves. They didn't do anything. Ever. Nothing but old broken toys. How do you forgive that, Tuyet?"

And then silence.

***

When Quan's parents first emigrated from Viet Nam, they ended up living in a house designed for college students. Their family shared the house with three sets of uncles and aunts on Quan's mother's side, each couple taking to one of five rooms. The fifth room—the master bedroom—was loaded with small cots and a crib so that all the children shared it. The parents all worked two shifts to stay afloat, and so it was the responsibility of the older children like Tuyet and their cousin Hung to take care of the others. Tuyet always joked that they lived like orphans, the way everyone was crammed into that room, these perfect geometric columns of cots. A few years later, their parents found work operating a printing press and bought a house.

Going to the printing press with his parents was Quan's most cherished memories of childhood; he loved watching them work. It was mesmerizing—Ma taking the prints on huge sheets of film and scanning them into a computer, Ba operating the glue binder and guillotine, Quan sitting on boxes watching the binder, a massive contraption of steel and oil, fold up millions of printed sheets into small tiny books. After a load of books was bound, Ba lined stacks of them up on the guillotine to slice off the stray edges. Mostly, the books were paperbound textbooks for high schools.

And when Binh started working summers at the press as a teenager, Quan waited with jittery anticipation every day for the stories Binh brought home, revealing a completely different side of their father. He told of Ba chatting with the other employees, laughing heartily at their jokes. According to Binh, Ba was considered the company prankster, always sneaking up and scaring people. One story involved Ba going into the layout designer's office and covering it in cellophane. Every inch. Walls, the chair, the computer, the desk, even each pen and pencil and his coffee mug were all individually cocooned in plastic film. It took two hours to clean up. The siblings were jealous when Binh returned with these stories. It was hard to not take personally.

***

Quan finally entered the house. He looked at his brother and sister in the kitchen. They wouldn't look at each other. He asked, "So what's this thing you found?"

Binh stood. "One second." He walked past Tuyet and Quan, and then up the stairs by the front door. He returned with a small black shoebox crushed under his left arm. They followed him from the kitchen into the living room, where Binh dropped the box onto the coffee table, sat down on the couch, and stared at its top. His hands were shaking. His eyes were wet.

Quan felt a lump in his throat. He looked at Tuyet, who was chewing on her lower lip, and saw that her eyes were drawn into sympathetic angles and as wet as Binh's. She felt it too—something dark pressing down on their brother, something awful and heavy. And then Binh sucked in a belly of air and lifted the top with a huge sigh, screwing his eyes up tight. Tuyet and Quan leaned in, gazed down. There were scattered scraps of paper and what looked like old photographs.

"I should've shown you earlier," said Binh.

Quan felt dizzy. It was like Binh had spun the world when he lifted the top away. Quan recognized their parents in one of the photographs, young and smiling with a child in their mother's lap. Tuyet asked, "Who's the kid? You think that's Hung?"

"It's not our cousin," said Binh forcefully. He picked a folded scrap of paper from the box and handed it to Tuyet. "This was in the music box when I took it apart."

Quan asked, "There was a note inside the music box?"

"All of this came from the toys."

"Wait, that's why you were taking them apart?"

"No, not at first," he answered. "I just wanted to know how they worked. And then I kept finding all these notes and photos." His voice croaked when he continued. "I thought Ba was giving me some kind of coded message. I wanted to piece it all together."

Tuyet looked up from the paper. "It's written in Vietnamese. Can you still read it?"

Quan took the note from Tuyet. He was the only sibling whom had bothered to keep practicing their language. The handwriting was sloppy, big and childish. All it said was, *Minh's third birthday gift to help him sleep and ease the nightmares.* The lines of Tuyet's face settled into confusion. Silence filled up time. Quan and Tuyet stared at their brother expectantly, too unsure and too afraid to ask questions.

After minutes, Binh explained, "I figured it out after the music box. All these little notes and drawings and photos created a narrative when I pieced it together. Tags that Ba put in all of the toys to remind him of what they were. I wasn't completely sure, but I asked our uncle, Cau Bon, about it in high school." For the first time, they heard the story of their parents.

***

Ma and Ba married early, seventeen and twenty respectively. They had their first child, whom they named Minh, the same year. Minh was four when the newly formed Viet Cong turned their attention to South Viet Nam. A grace period had been declared; any citizen that wanted nothing to do with a united Communist Viet Nam was free to leave. Ba had chosen to stay and fight—all Ma's brothers and sisters had already fled. In 1958, Ba's participation in the resistance was discovered. The Viet Cong came to the town in secret one night to raze the house. They weren't successful. The fire was put out before much harm was done, but Minh had died from smoke inhalation.

"Cau Bon said that Ma and Ba both suffered survivor's guilt. Ba most of all. He blamed himself for staying." Binh couldn't look at them. His face was buried in his palms.

Tuyet erupted. "You waited until now to tell us? Christ, Binh. I mean, just, Christ."

"I wanted them to tell us. Don't you think they should have been the ones? I thought for sure Ma would tell us any of the hundred nights in the hospital." He grunted. "God, if you're going to keep a secret like that, then you at least tell it on your deathbed, right?"

So that was why he went to see Ma more often than the others, why he wouldn't say anything to her when he did. He was waiting for her confession. Or trying to guilt her into it. Quan remembered after Ba's heart attack, how volatile Binh was.

They were grieving, and they needed him, and no one could speak to Binh for almost two years without him spitting curses, storming out, leaving a catastrophic boom of a door slam in his space. He must have thirsted for Ba's confession first, and then it became impossible. Ma was the only chance. For the first time, Quan saw his brother's rage as a hard black knot tightened up inside him instead of glowing red coals. Maybe Binh had kept it from them as a favor. Maybe he felt like Minh's replacement. Quan felt a sudden yearning to heal his brother. He wanted to touch his arm and tell him it was okay to be angry, that he was right, that the death of one child shouldn't invalidate parenting the rest. He didn't. They weren't that kind of family, although most days he really wished they were.

***

The house looked different in the morning. Tuyet and Quan woke early so they could drive together, and get to work packing away their parents' things, deciding who would get what and what would stay—Quan wanted Ba's chair and the photo albums, Tuyet wanted the laundry machine, maybe Binh wanted nothing at all. When they turned the corner, the house was painted in sunlight, each detail richly illuminated. Red brick walls veined with cracks sprouting more cracks. It reminded Quan of pictures of Mars in science magazines, a thirsty topography of rust and false rivers, cragged random lines of black empty space. And who really knew if there had once been water there?

Inside, they filled cardboard boxes up with all the empty artifacts of their parents. They were mostly silent—their movements ritualistic, the boxes sacrosanct. Tuyet asked, "Do you think we should sell?"

Quan shrugged. No one lived at the house. None of them wanted it. It was either rent or sell or keep the vast empty home just the way it was. Maybe Ba's ghost would lay in that recliner for ages more. "I don't know if I care," he said.

"You care," she said.

He nodded. "It's all we have left of them."

Binh came in the afternoon. The three siblings packed things up for hours into the evening. They didn't talk about last night. Most of the time they were silent, like dogs trained to not bark indoors. "Okay," Quan said. "We need to decide what we're going to do with this house. Today." Their eyes were on him, and he remembered all the times before, when he stood between them, when he tried to force talk, how they'd end up agreeing on some sort of compromise and weeks later, he'd discover they'd started arguing again in his absence. "Does it actually change anything? That we had a brother? That our parents didn't tell us?"

"It changes everything," Tuyet said. "Their lack of involvement in our lives could've been forgivable if they'd told us why. Now I feel cheated."

"So we're selling," said Binh.

"The hell we are! You should've told us sooner."

This set off another cascade of Tuyet and Binh arguing. Each stole a glance at Quan in intervals, expecting him to support one or the other. He didn't want to. He couldn't. Their anger was so hot and so ugly that Quan began to recede again.

Then the arguing abruptly stopped. Binh had a finger raised up to Tuyet. His eyebrows creased downward and he turned his head, casting his eyes toward every corner of the room again and again. He spun and looked and spun and looked until Tuyet asked, "What?"

"The music box," he said. "Have either of you packed it?"
They shook their heads.

"You kept it?" asked Quan.

"Of course I kept it!" Binh sped past his brother and dove
into the closet. He threw out shoes and boots and coats and scarves
in a rainbow of clothing. Next the board games. The hand vacuum.
The ironing board. "Where is it?"

Tuyet and Quan were looking at each other, and then looking at Binh. They didn't know what to do. They stood in the hall
watching him dig and dig into that closet. He went running upstairs, and they followed. They watched him frantically going into
each room, clawing out the contents of their closets, tearing out
the house's viscera for the old blue *Fur Elise* music box. He chanted, "Where is it? Where is it?" all the while, running back to each
closet again and again. He tore open each box we'd already packed
up, one box and then another, until all the contents of the home
lay scattered across the floor, forming mountains of clutter that ate
into the house's space.

Finally, he collapsed into the pile he had made on the
couch. His jaw clenched. Quan felt again that pressing urge to
sit beside and hug his brother. He willed himself to move toward
Binh, but nothing would happen. Tuyet and Quan sat watching
him until finally he got up and left. Quan was disappointed, when
he shut the door, that it didn't make a booming sound; he knew it
meant that everything was going to change between them now. He
felt an ache in his chest. Binh must have been expecting that once
they knew about Minh, they would have agreed with him.

"Did he remember to look in the basement?" Quan asked
Tuyet.

"No," she said, "I don't think so."

Quan started for the stairs. Tuyet's footsteps clicked behind
him. They dove down, into the boxes. He thought about Binh as
they searched—Binh in his car sliding over the roads toward home.
Angry, defeated, bitter. Quan thought about how he and Tuyet
locked up and became catatonic during Binh's desperate hunt and
how they only found the will to move when he turned away. This
was the best they could ever do, reaching out only when the other
wasn't looking.

END

Acknowledgements

I want to personally thank the following people who, without their contributions, support and inspiration, this book would not have been possible:

First, I cannot thank John Gosslee and Andrew Sullivan of C&R Press enough for the passion they have shown in bringing this book out to the public. Additionally, some of these stories have previously appeared in journals and magazines, so a deep thank you goes out to: Richard Peabody of Gargoyle Magazine for "The Message of My Skin;" Aaron Alford of Southern Humanities Review for "A Clear Sky Above the Clouds;" Paula Bomer and Adam Robinson with Sententia: The Journal for "Conversations with the Rest of the World;" Tom Dooley of Eclectica Magazine for "The Grinning Man;" Alexi Santi of Our Stories for "Prophecy;" April L. Ford of Digital Americana Magazine for "Beware of Dogma;" Justin L. Daugherty of Sundog Lit for "Once I Wed A White Woman;" Christine Hyung-Oak Lee with The Kartika Review for "The Golden Turtle God;" Brett Ortler of Knockout Literary Magazine for "Extinction with Residue Remaining."

I want to thank the faculty and my peers from the MFA program at Queens University of Charlotte for all their time spent helping me to hone these stories to their current form, especially Elissa Schappell, Jenny Offill, Steven Rinehart, Fred Leebron, Michael Kobre, Melissa Bashor, Pamela Powell, Naeem Murr, Jon Pineda, Matthew Maslowski, Anjali Enjeti, Mesha Maren, Ricky

Finlan, H. L. Nelson, and Walker Smart. Thank you to early readers of the stories and manuscripts: Christine Clark; Collin and Rachel Whitt; Johnny Le. To the communities of writers that gave me a sense of belonging, I give my undying gratitude, with a very special thanks to Lauren Groff, for her friendship and faith in me before there were any stories to speak of; to Laura van den Berg, for introducing me to the communities; to Mark Cugini and Laura Spencer for instantly welcoming me; to Amber Sparks; Michael Beeman; Jen Michalski; Matthew Salesses; and so many more. And, finally, thank you to Kirstin Margosian, who endured the terrible job of sitting with me as I mapped out the darkest territories of my mind developing these stories.

Each and every one of you has blessed my life in innumerable ways. Thank you so much. And I love you all.

About The Author

An Tran's fiction and non-fiction has appeared in the *Southern Humanities Review, Gargoyle Magazine, Carolina Quarterly, The Good Men Project,* and *Sundog Lit,* among others. His work has been identified as 'Notable' by the *Best American* series, nominated for the Pushcart Prize, and shortlisted for the Millions Writer Award. He received his MFA from Queens University of Charlotte and lives in Fairfax, VA.

OTHER C&R PRESS TITLES

FICTION

Spectrum
by Martin Ott

That Man in Our Lives
by Xu Xi

A History of the Cat In Nine Chapters or Less
by Anis Shivani

SHORT FICTION

Notes From the Mother Tongue
by An Tran

The Protester Has Been Released
by Janet Sarbanes

ESSAY AND CREATIVE NONFICTION

While You Were Gone
by Sybil Baker

Je suis l'autre: Essays and Interrogations
by Kristina Marie Darling

Death of Art
by Chris Campanioni

POETRY

Imagine Not Drowning
by Kelli Allen

Collected Lies and Love Poems
by John Reed

Tall as You are Tall Between Them
by Annie Christain

The Couple Who Fell to Earth
by Michelle Bitting

ANTHOLOGY

Zombies, Aliens, Cyborgs and the Ongoing Apocolypse
by Travis Denton and Katie Chaple

CHAPBOOKS

Notes from the Negro Side of the Moon
by Earl Braggs

A Hunger Called Music: A Verse History in Black Music
by Meredith Nnoka

Cuntstruck
by Kate Northrop

CPSIA information can be obtained
at www.ICGtesting.com
Printed in the USA
FSOW02n1337031117
40568FS